TROPIC DEATH

"Walrond was post-racial well before Barack Obama popularized the term. . . . There is something hopeful, I think, in the lurid thickets of [Walrond's] prose, a conviction that a 'Negro' writer can also be more than a Negro writer—that he can merely be an artist unconstrained by racial concerns."
—Alexander Nazaryan, *New York Daily News*

"Undeservedly out of print for over three decades, *Tropic Death* is a classic of the Harlem Renaissance that returns [to] the publisher who championed its author's unique voice in the 1920s—now with an illuminating introduction by Arnold Rampersad." —Bobbi Booker, *Philadelphia Tribune*

"In prose . . . tough as the hanging vines from which monkeys leap and chatter, and as unsentimental as blazing sun, ten intimate and body-touching pictures of the West Indies unroll themselves. There is nothing soft about this book. . . . The throbbing life and sun-bright hardness of these pages fascinate me. . . . And the ease and accuracy of Mr. Walrond's West Indian dialects support one in the belief that he knows very well the people of whom he writes."
—Langston Hughes, *New York Herald Tribune Books*

"Descriptively Walrond uses his flaming semi-tropical backgrounds, of metallic sea, gleaming sand, green jungle with a nervous, poignant intensity. . . . His sense of color in words is remarkable, also the audacity of verbal manipulation."

—Robert Herrick, *New Republic*

"Walrond dramatizes the present moment with overpowering actuality, yet he conveys a universe of implication. . . . A crowding, thrusting, contradictory and absorbingly interesting energy, as of life itself, is conveyed. . . . Walrond has brought a creative vision and a pleasingly bizarre skill with words to his undertaking. He has made a book which excites and disturbs, oppresses and enchants the reader. An unknown way of life has been enhanced and vivified to the point of all but beggaring the known mode of existence."

—*New York Times Book Review*

TROPIC DEATH

Eric Walrond

Introduction by Arnold Rampersad

LIVERIGHT PUBLISHING CORPORATION
A Division of W. W. Norton & Company
New York · London

For information about permission to reproduce selections from this book, write
to Permissions, Liveright Publishing Corporation, a division of W. W. Norton &
Company, Inc., 500 Fifth Avenue, New York, NY 10110

For information about special discounts for bulk purchases, please contact
W. W. Norton Special Sales at specialsales@wwnorton.com or 800-233-4830

Manufacturing by Courier Westford
Production manager: Devon Zahn

Library of Congress Cataloging-in-Publication Data

Walrond, Eric, 1898–1966.
Tropic death / Eric Walrond ; introduction by Arnold Rampersad.
p. cm.
ISBN 978-0-87140-335-3 (hardcover)
1. Barbados—Social life and customs—Fiction. 2. Panama—Social life and
customs—Fiction. I. Rampersad, Arnold. II. Title.
PS3545.A5826T76 2013
813'.52—dc23
2012033878

ISBN 978-0-87140-685-9 pbk.

Liveright Publishing Corporation
500 Fifth Avenue, New York, N.Y. 10110
www.wwnorton.com

W. W. Norton & Company Ltd.
Castle House, 75/76 Wells Street, London W1T 3QT

1 2 3 4 5 6 7 8 9 0

FOR *Jean, Dorothy,* AND *Lucille*

Contents

Eric Walrond's Tropic Death: An Introduction

Arnold Rampersad

When Eric Derwent Walrond arrived in New York City from Panama on June 30, 1918, he was no ordinary immigrant. Although only nineteen years old, he already embodied a dynamic Caribbean cosmopolitanism that few of his fellow migrants could match, as well as a developing literary sense that would set him apart from most of his contemporaries. These two major qualities would combine to remarkable effect in 1926 when the prestigious New York publisher Boni & Liveright brought out *Tropic Death*. This volume of stories would be one of the outstanding works of fiction of the so-called Harlem Renaissance, as well as an artistic achievement that deserves even wider acclaim.

Walrond was born in 1898 in British Guiana (now Guyana) in South America. His parents were immigrants from Barbados in the West Indies. In his early years, Walrond barely knew his father. Like thousands of other people from all over the Caribbean, his father (a tailor by trade) had gone to the Canal Zone lured by the money flowing from the vast

American-led construction project that in 1914 would link the Caribbean Sea to the Pacific Ocean. In 1906, after a fire burned down much of the capital of British Guiana, Walrond left with his mother to live in Barbados. Five years later, they moved from Barbados to Panama to rejoin his father. Eric Walrond stayed there until he was in his twentieth year, when he headed for New York.

In Panama, Walrond became fluent in Spanish. Drawn to writing, he began to work as a cub reporter for a Panama newspaper. A new world opened for him. The Canal Zone was the focal point of the wide variety of factors and forces that make up the Caribbean experience. While it offered poor blacks a ready way to make money, it also stood as a symbol of their often crude exploitation by North American and European interests, and by whites in general. But black and brown people hardly made up a solid cultural entity. They were a competitive, volatile amalgam of insular loyalties further complicated by tensions based on shadings of skin color and divisions according to money, class, education, and religion, among other considerations. All of these factors would breathe life and meaning into *Tropic Death*.

The variety of settings in *Tropic Death* speaks to Walrond's wide knowledge of the region. Of his ten stories, four ("Drought," "Panama Gold," "The Black Pin," and "The Vampire Bat") are set in Barbados. The setting of three stories ("The Wharf Rats," "The Palm Porch," and "Subjection") is the Canal Zone. One story ("The White Snake") takes place in British Guiana. Another ("The Yellow One") is set on a ship sailing from Honduras to Jamaica. Finally, the title story ("Tropic Death") takes place in three locations: the island of Barbados, aboard a ship bound for the Canal Zone, and then in Panama itself. Moreover, virtually every story brings together characters, often in conflict with one another, from different parts of the Caribbean.

Walrond arrived in New York at a particularly auspicious moment for blacks in the city. The mass movement of African Americans from the South to urban centers up North had led to unprecedented change, and nowhere more so than in New York. The Harlem Renaissance, which would blossom in the second half of the 1920s, was already in motion. For a young black immigrant with journalistic and literary interests, at least four major forces contended for influence. One was represented by the National Association for the Advancement of Colored People (NAACP), spearheaded by W. E. B. Du Bois, editor of its influential monthly magazine, *The Crisis*. The second was the black socialist movement, especially as featured in the monthly journal *The Messenger*, coedited by A. Philip Randolph and Chandler Owen. The third was the Universal Negro Improvement Association (UNIA), with its "Back to Africa" slogan, headed by the charismatic Jamaican political and cultural leader Marcus Garvey. Last of all was the varied world of white publications and publishing houses. Traditionally closed to black writers, these editors and publishers were beginning to open their eyes to more cosmopolitan vistas as the First World War drew to a close just as Walrond settled into New York.

Faithful to his Caribbean roots and his acute race consciousness, Walrond at first threw in his lot with Garvey after landing a reporter's job with his *Weekly Review*. He moved to Garvey's popular weekly *Negro World*, where he became an assistant and then an associate editor. However, his exposure to more cosmopolitan elements in New York cultural life led him away from Garvey. In 1925 he became business manager of *Opportunity: Journal of Negro Life*, edited by the sociologist Charles S. Johnson for the National Urban League. In addition to publishing in prominent journals aimed at blacks, such as *The Crisis*, *Opportunity*, and *The Messenger*, Walrond also saw his work appear in leading "white" journals as different as Henry Ford's *Dearborn Independent*, H. L. Mencken's *Smart Set*, and *The New Republic*.

Intelligent and personable, Walrond became friends with virtually all the stellar young writers of the Harlem Renaissance, such as the Jamaican-born Claude McKay, Zora Neale Hurston, Langston Hughes, Countee Cullen, and Wallace Thurman. Members of the older guard, including Du Bois, Charles S. Johnson, and Howard University professor Alain Locke, also welcomed him. In 1925, when Locke edited *The New Negro*, the definitive compendium about the blossoming renaissance, he made room for one of Walrond's stories ("The Palm Porch," which appears in revised form in *Tropic Death*). By this time, Walrond had rejected both propagandistic and tamely bourgeois strictures about art in favor of the approach that Langston Hughes would advocate in his landmark *Nation* essay of 1926, "The Negro Artist and the Racial Mountain." Black writers should never turn their backs on their racial origins, Hughes insisted, but neither should they surrender their freedom as artists to write exactly as they wished.

By 1926, the year *Tropic Death* appeared, Walrond knew how he wanted to write. His basic material would be the lives of the black, brown, and—in a few cases—white people of the Caribbean. His most profound sympathies would lie with poor blacks and browns, and his harshest criticism would be reserved for those people—white, brown, or black—who would exploit, censure, or disdain them. He underscored this commitment in a number of ways. One crucial way was in his dedication as an artist to capturing as accurately as possible the various dialects of the region. Like Mark Twain, who pointed proudly to the differences among the various dialects rendered in *Adventures of Huckleberry Finn*, Walrond took pride in his own command of regional dialects. He took pains to differentiate among, for example, Jamaican, Barbadian, and British Guianese speech. He wanted to accord each group what he saw as its proper measure of dignity.

Walrond's commitment to dialect makes *Tropic Death* difficult reading at times. To some extent, the collection is what literary critics have called a "local color" text, one self-consciously aimed at a superior, metropolitan audience. No doubt it is indeed a project in literary regionalism—as a result *Tropic Death* belongs with a number of key books by authors who practically revolutionized the idea of regionalism in America and elsewhere. Here one thinks of texts such as *Adventures of Huckleberry Finn*, James Joyce's *Dubliners*, Sherwood Anderson's *Winesburg, Ohio*, Jean Toomer's *Cane*, and William Faulkner's *The Sound and the Fury*. Probably the most important for Walrond was Toomer's *Cane* (1923), an extraordinary mélange of forms, including poetry, fiction, and drama, that sought to capture its author's tragic vision of a vanishing black South. Like Toomer, Walrond sought to fuse modernism with folk forms, the better to do justice to the complexity of black life as it lurched uncertainly into the twentieth century.

In some respects, the distinguishing mark of Walrond's art in *Tropic Death* is the sense of paradox enshrined in its title. Typically the tropics evoke images of vitality and fecundity, as well as a relaxed, even lazy, indulgence in the sensual world. In Walrond's work, however, the tropics are no paradise. The gorgeousness of nature is haunted by the specter of violence and death. It would be a mistake to attribute this degree of morbidity solely or even mainly to Walrond's hostility to social injustice. Indeed, only one story in *Tropic Death*, "Subjection," in which a black worker confronts a white U.S. Marine, comes close to being what is called "proletarian" or protest fiction. A sense of the essential tragedy of life goes hand in hand with Walrond's appreciation not only of tropical sensuality but also of the heroic quality of the lives of the black and brown people of the region.

Walrond's style—or styles—in *Tropic Death* in part reflects this sense of an inherent paradox or fascinating instability of meaning in his subject. He was not a conventional writer, nor did he wish to be one. Within certain limits, he was restless, imaginative, self-possessed, and fearless. He was alert to the possibilities of stream-of-consciousness writing, for example. Grief-stricken, a man in "Drought" listens to an autopsy being performed on his young daughter:

It came to Coggins in swirls. Autopsy. Noise comes in swirls. Pounding, pounding—dry Indian corn pounding. Ginger. Ginger being pounded in a mortar with a bright, new pestle. Pound, pound. And. Sawing. Butcher

shop. Cow foot is sawed that way. Stew—or tough hard
steak. Then the drilling—drilling—drilling to a stone
cutter's ears! Ox grizzle. Drilling into ox grizzle. . . .

The overall language of "Drought" epitomizes Walrond's way with words. Realism fuses with naturalism on the
one hand and with impressionism on the other; symbolism
works its stabilizing function; sentences break into fragments
under the pressure of modernist psychology applied to folk
consciousness; syntax, too, bends to accommodate the peculiar truths of Walrond's unusual vision of Caribbean reality.

Walrond respected the belief systems that sustained
ordinary people—from conventional religion to an almost
ineradicable faith in the "folk" or Gothic supernatural, in
obeah and "duppies" or spirits, in vampire bats that could
assume the form of black babies. Such is the case in "The
Vampire Bat," in which a man pays a terrible price for failing
to respect the "superstitions" by which the masses of common
people live. Naturalism, however, is central to the aesthetic
of *Tropic Death*. For Walrond, the Caribbean is a place of
extravagant natural beauty dominated by an almost impla-
cable sun that in "Drought," for example, tyrannizes the lives
of the people it watches over. The lands—islands or stretches
of coastal earth—are hemmed in by a sea that is both alluring and potentially malevolent, as when a shark attacks two
young men in "The Wharf Rats." Walrond's characters coex-
ist with sun and sea, but not as equals, much less superiors.
His people are under the dominion of natural forces that
stand in for a cosmic power that proclaims at every turn that
a persisting happiness is not possible. Life is both effulgent,

in that it reflects tropical richness, and also stringent, pinching. The people respond, above all, with a determination not only to endure but also to enjoy and, in the course of enjoying, perhaps to prevail in the face of suffering.

The social situation is fundamentally oppressive for those of the lower strata, which is to say for most of the people who inhabit the world of *Tropic Death*. Powerful commercial interests, epitomized by the foreigners who oversee the building of the great canal, loom almost satanically in the background, but among the various peoples history has left a contaminating residue of distrust and self-hatred. Conflicts over gradations of skin color in a world where white skin equals power and where nonwhites crave whiteness mar the psychological and spiritual landscape. In "Panama Gold," a mulatto woman looks down on a black-skinned man who just might be the answer to the loneliness that is draining her spirit even as she seems to be flourishing in self-sufficiency. In "The Yellow One," two men on board a ship clash violently over the implications of skin color with a degree of malevolence that mars even nature, as when from the ship there rises, at the end of the story, the sight of "the dead blue hills of Jamaica." "The Palm Porch" tells of a color-crazed Jamaican in Panama who prostitutes her daughters even as she would have them "rise" in the world by marrying white or light-skinned men.

For all the harassing elements of life in *Tropic Death*, however, Walrond subtly declares his admiration for the indomitable spirit of the common man and woman as they face both the oppressive social order and the overarching elements of fatalism and pessimism that afflict their lives.

Certainly theirs is a hard lot. In ending the title story of the collection, the vicariously autobiographical "Tropic Death," he allows the leprosy-afflicted father of the boy at the center of the tale to pronounce to the boy's mother a judgment on the world in which they live: "An' yo' mus' tek good cyah o' yo'self, heah Sarah, an' don't le' nobody tek exvantage o' yo', yo' heah, dis is a bad country—."

Walrond probably associated the tropics with a sense of ultimate personal futility in that he saw little or no future for himself anywhere in the region. He would never lose his sense of fascination with the Caribbean and especially with Panama. "I am spiritually a native of Panama," he would declare. "I owe the sincerest allegiance to it." Nevertheless, his fate was a life of vagabondage and exile, especially in Europe. Well received by critics in its day, *Tropic Death* turned out to be the high point of Walrond's career as a writer of fiction. Shortly after its appearance he applied to the John S. Guggenheim Foundation for a fellowship to travel in the Caribbean and produce, as he put it, "a series of novels and short stories of native life in the West Indies." He received both a year-long fellowship from the foundation and also an extension of six months.

After traveling in the West Indies in 1928 and 1929 and then spending about two years in France, Walrond settled down in England around 1931. He continued to write but never published another book. He remained in Great Britain until his death there in 1966.

ARNOLD RAMPERSAD
Stanford University

Bibliography

Parascandola, Louis J., ed. *"Winds Can Wake Up the Dead":*
An Eric Walrond Reader (Detroit, MI: Wayne State University Press, 1998).

Parascandola, Louis J., and Carl A. Wade, eds. *In Search of*
Asylum: The Later Writings of Eric Walrond (Gainesville: University Press of Florida, 2011).

TROPIC DEATH

Drought*

I

The whistle blew for eleven o'clock. Throats parched, grim,
sun-crazed blacks cutting stone on the white burning hillside
dropped with a clang the hot, dust-powdered drills and flew
up over the rugged edges of the horizon to descent into a dry,
waterless gut. Hunger—pricks at stomachs inured to brackish coffee and cassava pone—pressed on folk, joyful as rabbits
in a grassy ravine, wrenching themselves free of the lure of the
white earth. Helter-skelter dark, brilliant, black faces of West
Indian peasants moved along, in pain—the stiff tails of blue
denim coats, the hobble of chigger-cracked heels, the rhythm
of a stride . . . dissipating into the sun-stuffed void the radiant
forces of the incline.

The broad road—a boon to constables moping through
the dusk or on hot, bright mornings plowing up the thick,
adhesive marl on some seasonal chore, was distinguished by
a black, animate dot upon it.

It was Coggins Rum. On the way down he had stopped
for a tot—zigaboo word for tin cup—of water by the rock

* I wish to thank the editor of *The News Age* for permission to reprint
Drought.

engine. The driver, a buckra johnny—English white—sat on the waste box scooping with a fork handle the meat out of a young water cocoanut. An old straw hat, black, and its rim saggy by virtue of the moisture of sweating sun-fingers, served as a calabash for a ball of "cookoo"—corn meal, okras and butter stewed—roundly poised in its crown. By the buckra's side, a black girl stood, her lips pursed in an indifferent frown, paralyzed in the intense heat.

Passing by them Coggins' bare feet kicked up a cloud of the white marl dust and the girl shouted, "Mistah Rum, you gwine play de guitah tee nite, no?" Visions of Coggins—the sky a vivid crimson or blackly star-gemmed—on the stone step picking the guitar, picking it "with all his hand. . . ."

Promptly Coggins answered, "Come down and dance de fango fo' Coggins Rum and he are play for you."

> Bajan gal don't wash 'ar skin
> Till de rain come down. . . .

Grumblings. Pitch-black, to the "washed-out" buckra she was more than a bringer of victuals. The buckra's girl. It wasn't Sepia, Georgia, but a backwoods village in Barbadoes. "Didn't you bring me no molasses to pour in the rain-water?" the buckra asked, and the girl, sucking in her mouth, brought an ungovernable eye back to him.

Upon which Coggins, swallowing a hint, kept on his journey—noon-day pilgrimage—through the hot creeping marl.

Scorching—yet Coggins gayly sang:

O! you come with yo' cakes
Wit' yo' cakes an' yo' drinks
Ev'y collection boy ovah death!—
An' we go to wah—
We shall carry de name,
Bajan boys for—evah!

"It are funny," mused Coggins, clearing his throat, "Massa Braffit an' dat chiggah-foot gal. . . ."

He stopped and picked up a fern and pressed the back of it to his shiny ebon cheek. It left a white ferny imprint. Grown up, according to the ethics of the gap, Coggins was yet to it a "queer saht o' man," given to the picking of a guitar, and to cogitations, on the step after dark—indulging in an avowed juvenility.

Drunk with the fury of the sun Coggins carelessly swinging along cast an eye behind him—more of the boys from the quarry—overalled, shoeless, caps whose peaks wiggled on red, sun-red eyes . . . the eyes of the black sunburnt folk.

He always cast an eye behind him before he turned off the broad road into the gap.

Flaring up in the sun were the bright new shingles on the Dutch-style cottage of some Antigua folk. Away in a clump of hibiscus was a mansion, the color of bilgy water, owned by two English dowager maidens. In the gap rockstones shot up— obstacles for donkey carts to wrestle over at dusk. Rain-worms and flies gathered in muddy water platoons beside them.

"Yo' dam vagabond yo'!"

Coggins cursed his big toe. His big toe was blind. Help-

less thing . . . a blind big toe in broad daylight on a West
Indian road gap.

He paused, and gathered up the blind member. "Isn't
this a hell of a case fo' yo', sah?" A curve of flesh began to peel
from it. Pree-pree-pree. As if it were frying. Frying flesh. The
nail jerked out of place, hot, bright blood began to stream
from it. Around the spot white marl dust clung in grainy
cakes. Now, red, new blood squirted—spread over the whole
toe—and the dust became crimson.

Gently easing the toe back to the ground, Coggins
avoided the grass sticking up in the road and slowly picked
his way to the cabin.

"I stump me toe," he announced, "I stump me toe . . . woy
. . . woy."

"Go bring yo' pappy a tot o' water . . . Ada . . . quick."

Dusky brown Sissie took the gored member in her lap
and began to wipe the blood from it.

"Pappy stump he toe."

"Dem rocks in de gap . . ."

"Mine ain't got better yet, needer . . ."

"Hurry up, boy, and bring de lotion."

"Bring me de scissors, an' tek yo' fingers out o' yo' mout'
like yo' is starved out! Hey, yo', sah!"

". . . speakin' to you. Big boy lik' yo' suckin' yo' fingers. . . ."

Zip! Onion-colored slip of skin fluttered to the floor.
Rattah Grinah, the half-dead dog, cold dribbling from his
glassy blue eyes on to his freckled nose, moved inanimately
towards it. Fox terrier . . . shaggy . . . bony . . . scarcely able
to walk.

"Where is dat Beryl?" Coggins asked, sitting on the floor

with one leg over the other, and pouring the salt water over the crimsoning wadding.

"Outside, sah."

"Beryl!"

"Wha' yo' dey?"

"Wha' yo' doin' outside?"

"Answer me, girl!"

". . . Hey, yo' miss, answer yo' pappy!"

"Hard-ears girl! She been eatin' any mo' marl, Sissie?"

"She, Ada?"

"Sho', gal eatin' marl all de haftahnoon. . . ."

Pet, sugar—no more terms of endearment for Beryl. Impatient, Coggins, his big toe stuck up cautiously in the air—inciting Rattah to indolent curiosity—moved past Sissie, past Ada past Rufus to the rear of the cabin.

II

Yesterday, at noon . . . a roasting sun smote Coggins. Liquid . . . fluid . . . drought. Solder. Heat and juice of fruit . . . juice of roasting *cashews*.

It whelmed Coggins. The dry season was at its height. Praying to the Lord to send rain, black peons gathered on the rumps of breadfruit or cherry trees in abject supplication.

Crawling along the road to the gap, Coggins gasped at the consequences of the sun's wretched fury. There, where canes spread over with their dark rich foliage into the dust-laden road, the village dogs, hunting for eggs to suck, fowls to kill, paused amidst the yellow stalks of cork-dry canes to pant, or drop, exhausted, sun-smitten.

The sun had robbed the land of its juice, squeezed it dry. Star apples, sugar apples, husks, transparent on the dry sleepy trees. Savagely prowling through the orchards blackbirds stopped at nothing. . . . Turtle doves rifled the pods of green peas and purple beans and even the indigestible Brazilian *bonavis*. Potato vines, yellow as the leaves of autumn, severed from their roots by the pressure of the sun, stood on the ground, the wind's eager prey. Undug, stemless—peanuts, carrots—seeking balm, relief, the caress of a passing wind, shot dead unlustered eyes up through sun-etched cracks in the hard, brittle soil. The sugar corn went to the birds. Ripening prematurely, breadfruits fell swiftly on the hard naked earth, half ripe, good only for fritters. . . . Fell in spatters . . . and the hungry dogs, elbowing the children, lapped up the yellow-mellow fruit.

His sight impaired by the livid sun, Coggins turned hungry eyes to the soil. Empty corn stalks . . . blackbirds at work. . . .

Along the water course, bushy palms shading it, frogs gasped for air, their white breasts like fowls, soft and palpitating. The water in the drains sopped up, they sprang at flies, mosquitoes . . . wrangled over a mite.

It was a dizzy spectacle and the black peons were praying to God to send rain. Coggins drew back. . . .

Asking God to send rain . . . why? Where was the rain? Barreled up there in the clouds? Odd! Invariably, when the ponds and drains and rivers dried up they sank on their knees asking God to pour the water out of the sky. . . . Odd . . . water in the sky. . . .

The sun! It wrung toll of the earth. It had its effect on

Coggins. It made the black stone cutter's face blacker. Strong tropic suns make black skins blacker. . . .

At the quarry it became whiter and the color of dark things generally grew darker. Similarly, with white ones—it gave them a whiter hue. Coggins and the quarry. Coggins and the marl. Coggins and the marl road.

Beryl in the marl road. Six years old; possessing a one-piece frock, no hat, no shoes.

Brown Beryl . . . the only one of the Rum children who wasn't black as sin. Strange . . . Yellow Beryl. It happens that way sometimes. Both Coggins and Sissie were unrelievably black. Still Beryl came a shade lighter. "Dat am nuttin'," Sissie had replied to Coggins' intimately naïve query, "is yo' drunk dat yo' can't fomembah me sistah-in-law what had a white picknee fo' 'ar naygeh man? Yo' don't fomembah, no?" Light-skinned Beryl. . . .

It happens that way sometimes.

Victim of the sun—a bright spot under its singeing mask—Beryl hesitated at Coggins' approach. Her little brown hands flew behind her back.

"Eatin' marl again," Coggins admonished, "eatin' marl again, you little vagabon'!"

On the day before he had had to chastise her for sifting the stone dust and eating it.

"You're too hard ears," Coggins shouted, slapping her hands, "you're too hard ears."

Coggins turned into the gap for home, dragging her by the hand. He was too angry to speak . . . too agitated.

Avoiding the jagged rocks in the gap, Beryl, her little body lost in the crocus bag frock jutting her skinny shoul-

ders, began to cry. A gulping sensation came to Coggins
when he saw Beryl crying. When Beryl cried, he felt like crying, too. . . .

But he sternly heaped invective upon her. "Marl'll make
yo' sick . . . tie up yo' guts, too. Tie up yo' guts like green gua-
vas. Don't eat it, yo' hear, don't eat no mo' marl. . . ."

No sooner had they reached home than Sissie began.
"Eatin' marl again, like yo' is starved out," she landed a clout
on Beryl's uncombed head. "Go under de bed an' lay down
befo' I crack yo' cocoanut. . . ."

Running a house on a dry-rot herring bone, a pint of
stale, yellowless corn meal, a few spuds, yet proud, thumping
the children around for eating scraps, for eating food cooked
by hands other than hers . . . Sissie. . . .

"Don't talk to de child like dat, Sissie."

"Oh, go 'long you, always tryin' to prevent me from
beatin' them. When she get sick who gwine tend she? Me or
you? Man, go 'bout yo' business."

Beryl crawled meekly under the bed. Ada, a bigger girl—
fourteen and "ownwayish"—shot a look of composed neu-
trality at Rufus—a sulky, cry-cry, suck-finger boy nearing
twenty—Big Head Rufus.

"Serve she right," Rufus murmured.

"Nobody ain't gwine beat me with a hairbrush. I know
dat." One leg on top of the other, Ada, down on the floor,
grew impatient at Sissie's languor in preparing the food. . . .

Coggins came in at eleven to dinner. Ada and Rufus did
likewise. The rest of the day they spent killing birds with
stones fired from slingshots; climbing neighbors' trees in
search of birds' nests; going to the old French ruins to dig

out, with the puny aid of Rattah Grinah, a stray mongoose
or to rob of its prize some canary-catching cat; digging holes
in the rocky gap or on the brink of drains and stuffing them
with paper and gunpowder stolen from the Rum canister
and lighting it with a match. Dynamiting! Picking up hollow
pieces of iron pipe, scratching a hole on top of them, towards
one end, and ramming them with more gunpowder and
stones and brown paper, and with a pyramid of gunpowder
moistened with spit for a squib, leveling them at snipes or
sparrows. Touch bams.

"Well, Sissie, what yo' got fo' eat today?"

"Cookoo, what yo' think Ah are have?"

"Lawd, mo' o' dat corn mash. Mo' o' dat prison gruel.
People would t'ink a man is a horse!" . . . a restless crossing of
scaly, marl-white legs in the corner.

"Any salt fish?"

"Wha' Ah is to get if from?"

"Herrin'?"

"You t'ink I must be pick up money. Wha' you expect
mah to get it from, wit' butter an' lard so dear, an' sugar four
cents a pound. Yo' must be expect me to steal."

"Well, I ain't mean no harm. . . ."

"Hey, this man muss be crazy. You forget I ain't workin'
ni, yo' forget dat I can't even get water to drink, much mo'
grow onions or green peas. Look outside. Look in the yard.
Look at the parsley vines."

Formerly things grew under the window or near the
tamarind trees, fed by the used water or the swill, yams,
potatoes, lettuce. . . .

Going to the door, Coggins paused. A "forty-leg" was

working its way into the craw of the last of the rum hens. "Lahd 'a' massie. . . ." Leaping to the rescue, Coggins slit the hen's craw—undigested corn spilled out—and ground the surfeited centipede underfoot.

"Now we got to eat this," and he strung the bleeding hen up on a nail by the side of the door, out of poor Rattah Grinah's blinking reach. . . .

Unrestrained rejoicing on the floor.

Coggins ate. It was hot—hot food. It fused life into his body. It rammed the dust which had gathered in his throat at the quarry so far down into his stomach that he was unaware of its presence. And to eat food that had butter on it was a luxury. Coggins sucked up every grain of it.

"Hey, Ada."

"Rufus, tek this."

"Where is dat Miss Beryl?"

"Under de bed, m'm."

"Beryl. . . ."

"Yassum. . . ."

Unweeping, Beryl, barely saving her skull, shot up from underneath the bed. Over Ada's obstreperous toes, over Rufus' by the side of Coggins, she had to pass to get the proffered dish.

"Take it quick!"

Saying not a word, Beryl took it and, sliding down beside it, deposited it upon the floor beside Coggins.

"You mustn't eat any more marl, yo' hear?" he turned to her. "It will make yo' belly hard."

"Yes . . . pappy."

Throwing eyes up at him—white, shiny, appealing—

Beryl guided the food into her mouth. The hand that did the act was still white with the dust of the marl. All up along the elbow. Even around her little mouth the white, telltale marks remained.

Drying the bowl of the last bit of grease, Coggins was completely absorbed in his task. He could hear Sissie scraping the iron pot and trying to fling from the spoon the stiff, over-cooked corn meal which had stuck to it. Scraping the pan of its very bottom, Ada and Rufus fought like two mad dogs.

"You, Miss Ada, yo' better don't bore a hole in dat pan, gimme heah!"

"But, Mahmie, I ain't finish."

Picking at her food, Beryl, the dainty one, ate sparingly. . . .

Once a day the Rums ate. At dusk, curve of crimson gold in the sensuous tropic sky, they had tea. English to a degree, it was a rite absurdly regal. Pauperized native blacks clung to the utmost vestiges of the Crown. Too, it was more than a notion for a black cane hole digger to face the turmoil of a hoe or fork or "bill"—zigaboo word for cutlass—on a bare cup of molasses coffee.

III

"Lahd 'a' massie. . . ."

"Wha' a mattah, Coggins?"

"Say something, no!"

"Massie, come hay, an' see de gal picknee."

". . . open yo' mout' no, what's a mattah?"

Coggins flew to the rainwater keg. Knocked the swizzle

stick—relic of Sissie's pop manufactures—behind it, tilting over the empty keg.

"Get up, Beryl, get up, wha' a mattah, sick?"

"Lif' she up, pappy."

"Yo' move out o' de way, Mistah Rufus befo'. . . ."

"Don't, Sissie, don't lick she!"

"Gal playin' sick! Gal only playin' sick, dat what de mattah wit' she. Gal only playin' sick. Get up yo' miss!"

"God—don't, Sissie, leave she alone."

"Go back, every dam one o' yo', all yo' gwine get in de way."

Beryl, little naked brown legs apart, was flat upon the hard, bare earth. The dog, perhaps, or the echo of some fugitive wind had blown up her little crocus bag dress. It lay like a cocoanut flapjack on her stomach. . . .

"Bring she inside, Coggins, wait I gwine fix de bed."

Mahogany bed . . . West Indian peasants sporting a mahogany bed; canopied with a dusty grimy slice of cheesecloth. . . .

Coggins stood up by the lamp on the wall, looking on at Sissie prying up Beryl's eyelids.

"Open yo' eyes . . . open yo' eyes . . . betcha the little vagabon' is playin' sick."

Indolently Coggins stirred. A fist shot up—then down. "Move, Sissie, befo' Ah hit yo'." The woman dodged.

"Always wantin' fo' hit me fo' nuttin', like I is any picknee."

". . . anybody hear this woman would think. . . ."

"I ain't gwine stand for it, yes, I ain't gwine. . . ."

"Shut up, yo' old hard-hearted wretch! Shut up befo' I tump yo' down!" . . . Swept aside, one arm in a parrying attitude . . . backing, backing toward the larder over the lamp. . . .

Coggins peered back at the unbreathing child. A shade of compassion stole over Sissie. "Put dis to 'er nose, Coggins, and see what'll happen." Assafetida, bits of red cloth. . . .

Last year Rufus, the sickliest of the lot, had had the measles and the parish doctor had ordered her to tie a red piece of flannel around his neck. . . .

She stuffed the red flannel into Coggins' hand. "Try dat," she said, and stepped back.

Brow wrinkled in cogitation, Coggins—space cleared for action—denuded the child. "How it ah rise! How 'er belly a go up in de year!"

Bright wood; bright mahogany wood, expertly shellacked and laid out in the sun to dry, not unlike it. Beryl's stomach, a light brown tint, grew bit by bit shiny. It rose; round and bright, higher and higher. They had never seen one so none of them thought of wind-filling balloons. Beryl's stomach resembled a wind-filling balloon.

Then—

"She too hard ears," Sissie declared, "she won't lissen to she pappy, she too hard ears."

Dusk came. Country folk, tired, soggy, sleepy, staggering in from "town"—depressed by the market quotations on Bantam cocks—hollowed howdy-do to Coggins, on the stone step, waiting.

Rufus and Ada strangely forgot to go down to the hydrant to bathe their feet. It had been passion with Coggins. "Nasty feet breed disease he had said, "you Mistah Rufus, wash yo' foot befo' yo' go to sleep. An' yo', too, Miss Ada, I'm speaking to yo', gal, yo' hear me? Tak' yo' mouth off o' go 'head, befo' Ah box it off. . . ."

Inwardly glad of the escape, Ada and Rufus sat not by Coggins out on the stone step, but down below the cabin, on the edge of a stone overlooking an empty pond, pitching rocks at the frog and crickets screaming in the early dusk.

The freckled-face old buckra physician paused before the light and held up something to it . . .

"Marl . . . marl . . . dust. . . ."

It came to Coggins in swirls. Autopsy. Noise comes in swirls. Pounding, pounding—dry Indian corn pounding. Ginger. Ginger being pounded in a mortar with a bright, new pestle. Pound, pound. And. Sawing. Butcher shop. Cow foot is sawed that way. Stew—or tough hard steak. Then the drilling—drilling—drilling to a stone cutter's ears. Ox grizzle. Drilling into ox grizzle. . . .

"Too bad, Coggins," the doctor said, "too bad, to lose yo' dawtah. . . ."

In a haze it came to Coggins. Inertia swept over him. He saw the old duffer climb into his buggy, tug at the reins of his sickly old nag and slowly drive down the rocky gap and disappear into the night.

Inside, Sissie, curious, held things up to the light. "Come," she said to Coggins, "and see what 'im take out a' 'ar. Come an' see de marl. . . ."

And Coggins slowly answered, "Sissie—if yo' know what is good fo' yo'self, you bes' leave dem stones alone."

Panama Gold

~~~~~~

I

The sun was slowly dying. Ella, a switch in her hand, rounded
up her chicks. Cocks came proudly in, puffed by poise and
conquest; hens, agitated, jealous of their young, clucked in—
furious at the disappearance of a one-eyed one caught by the
leg and dragged down the hole of a mongoose.

"Yo' go up dere, an' behave yo'self."

Swish, swish, swish . . . "Ah know you had to be last, yo'
rascal yo' . . . jump inside!" Guinea fowl, swifter than a hare,
wild as any of the gap's tabbies.

The wind subsided. Butter fish clung to the sky . . .
fish in the sky . . . mullets, gar fish, butter fish. Fish—blue,
gold, black, orange—tossing on a sea, floundering around in
God's sky. Fishermen at Low'rd set their nets by the twilight
visions, mirrored in the sky, of the lore rolling drunk on the
sea's bottom. They were dark sea rats streaming out at twilight to embark on some intrepid quest.

She would be alone at dusk, cooking, mixing flour or
tasting broth. . . . "Why taste it, why? If no fo' me alone?"
Yampies, eddoes, plantains . . .

"De Bajan man him say," Ella smiled, "'plantain an' salt
fish me don't want 'um, an' de Mud-head man him say, me

wish me had 'um, me wish me had 'um. . . .'" And moisture came to Ella's laughing eyes.

From the plantains to the corn and the flour dumplings. . . . "One o' dem would knock a man in a cock hat," she observed . . . a man . . . a man. . . .

All of a sudden a problem arose, "Gahd, I ain't got a bit o' salt in de house. No, sah," she cried frantically, "me can't stand no fresh food—me muss get a pinch o' salt."

II

"Yo' mahmie inside, Capadosia?" Ella paused before the Dalrimple cabin. Even the mangy brindle pup with his ears sticking sickly up row-rowed hoarsely after the spunky downpour of rain.

"I is talkin' to you, girl!"

And Capadosia, still pricking the chigger fested in her thumb, hollowed, "Mahmie!"

"Don't tu'n yo' back 'pon me, girl, befo' I tell yo' mahmie!" Unruly Capadosia!

"Capadosia, what is it?"

"Miss Heath, heah, mum, she want yo'. . . ."

Skimpy-legged Capadosia, the color of a warm chestnut, freckles dominant on her rude, glazed, hard little face.

"Hey, dese chilrun, Lizzie. . . ."

Ella stepped over to Capadosia's mother. "Hey, I ask de gal if she mahmie home an' Lizzie, yo' know what she tell ma, why de little rapscallion tu'n me she back side an' didn't even say ax yo' pardin."

"Come in heah, miss, come in heah an' tu'n round. Ax

Miss Heath pardin! Ax she! yo' won't—yo' wretch! Vagabond! Take dat, an' dat, an' dat—shut up, I sez. Shut up, befo' I box ev'y one o' dem teets down yo' t'roat! Didn't I tell yo' not to be rude, shut up, yes—didn't I tell yo' not to be onmannerly to people, dat yo' must respect de neighbors? Like she ain't got no manners! Shut up, I sez, befo' I hamstring yo', yo' little whelp!"

"Dese gal picknees nowadays is 'nouf to send yo' to de madhouse! Hey, but Lizzie, what we gwine do wit' de chilrun, ni? Ev'y day dey is gettin' wussah an' wussah."

"Lord only knows, soulee gal, dat Miss Capadosia, yo' wait till she pappy come home. He gwine beat she fo' true."

Ella drew near the cabin door; near enough to be able to spy, through the blue smoke of Lizzie Dalrimple's cooking, Capadosia cutting her eyes at her and murmuring, "come complainin' 'pon me—de old hag—why she don't go 'n get sheself a man?"

"An' how yo', ni," cried Ella, turning to Lizzie and coloring brightly, "how yo'?"

"Oh, so so, soulee gal, I still got de rheumaticks in me leg."

"Yo' ain't doin' not'ing far-rit, no? Hey, gal yo' ain't frighten, no? Yo' ain't afraid o' de horspitral, no?"

"Come in an' sit down, Ella, an' res' yo'self."

"Don't put yo'self out o' de way, Lizzie, on account o' me. I wus jus' gwine ask yo' to len' me a pinch o' salt when dat gal chile o' yours skin up she behin' at me. A body can't even talk to chilrun nowadays."

"Tell yo' de troot, Ella," Lizzie answered, "I jus' use de las' drop meself to sweeten Christian's coffee. It make he coffee taste good."

"An' how's Christian, soulee?"

"Oh, so so, chile."

"He still at de quarry?"

"Yes, soul."

"Well, I gwine go back down de gap. I lef' de pot boilin'.'"

"Yes, soulee gal, I jus' shell de bonavis an' put dem in, an' in course de dumplings will tek long fo' swell up."

"Which kahl to mine dat las' ebenin' Christian bring home a bag o' soup-crabs from Miss Foulkes, de buckra. She are always givin' him soup meat, or pepper soup, or crab fo' soup, fo' tek' 'way. How-somevah, dem crabs is so nice, chile, I nevah taste nothin' like dem in all me bawn days."

"We usta catch dem in Low'rd, too—but I don't like dem. Giv' me de belly ache."

"Why yo' don't go up de road an' get a bag o' salt?"

"Up whey?"

"Up at Missah Poyah's shop."

"Missah who?"

"Missah Poyah, no."

"Who 'im are—whey he come from?"

"Palama, soul."

"Palama?"

"Yes."

"An' wha' he doin' heah?"

"He open a shop, soulee."

"Oh, I see."

"Yes, chile, he are a Palama man."

"Well, I must be goin' den," Ella drew the shawl around her shoulders. "I must go see disyah Poyah."

"An' oh, Ella, he got one leg—"

"Yo' don't say!"

"Deed he is! Got it cut off on de canal—"

"I gwine 'long now. Got to go back . . . leave me pot boilin' . . . got to go back an' eat me fresh food."

III

Aftermath—green aftermath.

The gap gave up the scurvy ghost. In balloons of steaming froth, the fog of drought and heat, which had settled over the gap for the entire summer, bore its way over the craggy tips of Low'rd to the red, brewing sea beyond.

Splashes of rain—a swift transfusion. The earth murmured under it; lay tense, groaning, swollen, like a woman in toil, with the burden of its inheritance. Gold and green and yellow things, near-ripe, sent up tall, nodding fronds to trumpet the bursting of the dawn.

Dawn cast a greenish gold over the gap. Over the jagged stones donkey carts slipped, wheels stuck in mud. Men got down to coax their beasts out of the muddy gutter. Gone the dust. Red mud flowed over the land. Red mud—good for beans and potatoes—crawled up the legs of dusky West Indian peasant women, up the hoofs of townbound cattle.

Once more the peewits sang. Strange—the way they found their way back to the tip-top ends of guava or breadfruit or pine. Gobbling turkeys and fowls, fond of their new, egg-crusted young, proudly stepped out of coops, traversing the broad marl highway. Worms swarmed into their paths to be devoured; plenty to go round. Mixed with the rain the marl dust made a hard resilient road.

The wind tossed the lanky guava tree. Scudding pop-corn—white, yellow, crimson pink guava buds blew upon the ground. Forwards and backwards the wind tossed the guava tree. It shook buds and blossoms on the ground—moist, unforked, ground—on Ella Heath's lap, in her black, plente-ous hair, in the water she was drawing from the well. Guava buds fell in Ella's bucket, and she liked it. They gave flavor to the water. All of nature gave flavor to Ella, wrought a magic color in Ella's life. Green, wavy moss—rhubarb moss—at the bottom of the frog-harboring well, with fern and broad leaf sprawled along its ribs; brought color to the water, gave body flavor to it. Gave the water a tang.

Cast up on a bare half acre of land, Ella came to know the use of green, virgin things. Ore; green ore—spread over the land. Riotously nature peopled the earth about her. In front of her cabin door there was a water course. It was filled with sparrow grass. A wild, mad, hectic green—the green of young sugar canes. Up and down the gap, horses, donkeys, ring-horned goats, on the way to Bridgetown to be raced, tugged at their tethers, crazy to eat up Ella's sparrow grass. It tempted the oxen carting tremulous loads of salty sugar cane grown on the swampy seaside of Barbadoes—tempted sheep, oracular, voiceless, dog-shy sheep bewilderedly on the road to market—tempted hens frizzly with the pip, and leaping, lap-eared dogs.

Ella had come from Low'rd—the Lower Side—that dinky bar of salty black earth jutting out to sea on the east-ernmost tip of Barbadoes. From Low'rd Ella had brought a donkey cart load of sea crab shells, horns, conchs, rose and orange and crimson hued, and set them in rows between the blazing hibiscus and chrysanthemum along the walk.

Inexhaustible stems of green sprang up around Ella's domain. It'd take five years to mature, but she had planted a cocoanut tree on the northern-most wing of the cabin. Half an acre of land, but it was no trifling stake. Inch by inch green overspread it. Corn, okras, gunga peas, eddoes, *tannias,* tomatoes—in such a world Ella moved.

As if she were on an immemorial lark, Ella experimented with the green froth of the earth. One day she was grafting a pine and breadfruit. Standing, "jooking" a foreign stalk in—tamarind, star apple, almond—and strapping it into the gummy gash dug into the tree's side.

Similarly, with the pigeons and the ground doves. Pigeons at sunrise on a soapbox coop set on top the latrine cooing:

> A rooka ta coo
> A rooka ta coo
> My wife is just as good as you
> Good as you
> Good as you

to sherbet-winged doves on the cabin roof—in spite of Ella's scissors. And rabbits; red-eyed ones white and shy, Ella'd set in the thick sparrow grass, guarded over by Jit, the dog, to play and frolic. Sometimes, unmoved by their genetic dissimilarity, Ella'd use drastic, aggressive methods. . . .

Sows fared prodigiously at the hands of Ella. She filled huge, fat-stinking troughs of slime for them. Ella's boars grew tusks of flint-like ivory. Vicious, stiff-haired boars who ate up the sow's young, frothed at the mouth at Jit's approach, tried to stick their snouts between Ella's legs whenever she ventured in the pen.

Under Ella's tutelage the one cow she owned streamed milk. From fat luscious udders filled skillet after skillet. . . .

Gay, lonely girl, her bare arms yellow in the blazing February sun, the words of a West Indian madrigal issued from her lips:

> Do Mistah Bee don't chase me 'way
> Fo' de gals nex' do' will laugh at me
> Break me han' but let me stan'
> Break me han' but let me stan'. . . .

Ella poured the water in a skillet. Guava buds in the water—honey in guava buds.

All around it was dark. Gravel assailed her feet. A moon worked its way through a welter of thick black clouds to soar untrammeled in the phosphorescent sky. Marl dust assailed Ella's unshod feet.

Under the evergreen big barnacled roots stood up like a mass of sleeping crocodiles—and Ella grew tired, and like blacks on a dark country road at night, began to sing

> Do Mistah Bee don't chase me 'way

The broad road led to the world. Beyond Black Rock, beyond St. Michael's to Eagle Hall Corner, and Bridgetown. Along it traders from Low'rd, in landaux and victorias and oxcarts, sped to barter sea eggs

> Sea egg, sea egg
> Tittee Ann tan tan!

Evergreen leaves fell swirling through the dusk upon Ella's face. She brushed them away, and into her untutored mind came a legend. "Sh, carrion crow," she cried, "me no dead yet." The evergreen leaves, caressing her face, brought it vividly to her. . . . "Sh, carrion crow, me no dead yet." An old Dutch Guianese had uttered the ghastly words. Black Portuguese legend. . . . For sticking his hand in a pork barrel in a Portuguese grocer's shop, a Negro had been caught and whisked off to a dark spot in the woods. His hands had been cut off and he had been buried alive, with only his head sticking out of the ground. That had happened at night. In the morning the crows had come to gouge the eyes out of his head. "Sh, carrion crow, me no dead yet. . . ." Evergreen leaves on Ella's face . . . crows swirling around the head of a body buried on the Guiana mound. . . .

"Dis muss be it," Ella murmured.

Up a greasy embankment, one more leap, and Ella paused, breathing hard. Words—male words—vied with the wind for position in her alert consciousness.

Voices—

". . . I mek dem pay me! Deed I dids! Says to dem, 'pay me, or be Christ you'll stan' de consequences!' 'Pay me,' I says, 'or I'll sick de British bulldog on all yo' Omericans!'"

"An' dey pay yo' fas' enough, didn' dey?"

"Pay me? Man, yo' should o' see how fas' dey pay me! Pay me fas' enough, indeed! Five hundred pounds! Ev'y blind cent! Man, I wuz ready to sick Nelson heself 'pon dem. At a moment's notice, me an' de council wuz gettin' ready fo' ramsack de Isthmus and shoot up de whole blasted locks! Hell wit' de Canal! We wuz gwine blow up de dam, cut down de wireless station an' breck up de gubment house! If dey didn't pay me fo' my foot!"

"Yo' handle dem fo' true, didn't yo'?"

"Man, don't tahlk! Shut yo' mout'! Handle dem? Dat am not all de troot. I swallow dem up! Swallow dem up like a salipentah! Sha'? Man, let me tell yo' something. I let dem understand quick enough dat I wuz a Englishman and not a bleddy American nigger! A' Englishman—big distinction in dat, Bruing! An' dat dey couldn't do as dey bleddy well please wit' a subject o' de King! Whuh? I carry on like a rattlesnake. Carry on like a true Bimshah! Heah I wuz losin' my foot fo' dem wit' dere bleddy canal an' dey come tellin' me dey wuzn't to blame, dat nobody wuz to blame, dat de engine wuz gwine slow an' dat I wuz musta been layin' down on de job. Hear dem Americans, ni? Layin' down on de job, hear dat, Bruing? And wuzzahmo' dey say dat why I didn't ketch holt o' de cow-katcher an' fling meself outa de way! Wha', man, dah t'ing knock me onconscience! I didn't even know I wuz hit! Dere I wuz oilin' de switch—oilin' de switch an' de nex' t'ing yo' know I wuz in de horspitral at Ancong wit' one foot cut off."

Pipes were being smoked . . . stinking tobacco smote Ella. Green tobacco leaves burning in rotting corncob pipes.

Sugar, snuff, codfish, lard oil, sweet oil, corn, rum, kerosene—were the ingredients of one grand symphonic smell.

"Giv' me a bag o' salt an' a package o' senna."

"Are dat yo', Miss Ella?"

"Yes, it am me."

She turned. Perched on an old biscuit barrel was Pettit Bruin, the village idiot, smoking a pipe which exuded an odor of burning cow dung.

"Howdy do, Mistah Bruing, how de worle a treat yo'?"

"Oh, so so, gal."

Ella's eyes deserted the old man to light upon the shop-keeper sticking his black veiny hand in the brine for the salt beef, his back to her. With a stab to the breast, she noted the protrudent tip of the cork leg. . . .

"Anything else, miss?" he asked, the brine dripping from his salt-crusted arm.

"Gahd, he are black in troot," Ella, mulatto Ella observed to herself; then aloud, "bettah giv' me a gill o' bakin' soda, I might wan' to make a cake."

"Look out dey, Poyah," mumbled Bruin, "gwine bring down dat salmon tin 'pon yo' head too."

"Oh dat can't hit me," Poyer replied, lowering the baking powder on the tip of the hook. "I's a man, man."

He faced Ella, piling up the goods on the counter. "I's a man, man," he said, meeting Ella's frosting eyes. "I wuz a brakesman in Palama, don' fomembah dat. I wuz de bes' train hooper on de Isthmus!"

"Count up de bill, quick!" Ella hastened, putting a six-pence on the counter. "It a get dark."

"Frighten fo' duppies?" Poyer said, a suggestion of teasing and mockery in his voice.

Island bugaboo. . . . "Who, me?" Ella's eye blazed, "I ain't frighten fo' de livin' much mo' de dead!"

"T'ink I is any cry-cry ooman, t'ink I is any cry-cry ooman—yo' lie!"

On the way back up the gap Ella felt unforgivingly warm in the temples at the very idea of Poyer's thinking she was afraid of ghosts. "Like I is any mamby-pamby ooman, like I ain't usta to takin' care o' meself."

Six days passed. Ella stuck a pig and corned the meat. The sapodillas ripened. Shaddocks—tropical grapefruits—filled donkey cart after donkey cart going through the gap to Eagle Hall Corner. Often as the sun rose showers fell. And then a visitor came—with a peg-step. . . .

It was dark when he came. He was perspiring furiously. He was one of those black men whose faces present an onion-like sheen, and upon whose brow and flabby jaws little fester-bright pimples stand out with a plaguing glitter.

He met Ella by the side of the well, binding up the spurs of a pugnacious game cock.

"I shut up de shop," he said abruptly, "why don't yo' come an' buy from me any mo'?"

"Hey, wha' yo' t'ink o' dat? Wha' wuz I doin' befo' yo' come along? Yo' t'ink I was starvin'? I look like I is starved out? Look at me good! We had plenty shops befo' yo' come along, bo."

"I taught—"

"Wha' yo' are taught? Yo' must be a funny man. Hey, yo' lock up yo' shop fi' come aftah one customah! Dat are a funny business."

"Bruing is dere—besides, it are good business."

"Tell me, how it are good business? Explain yo'self."

"Fo' me it are."

"Me can't see it, sah, furdah mo, I gwine ask yo' fo' excuse me, I got de chicken dem fo' feed."

"Wait—befo' yo' go, Ella—Miss Ella, yo' don't seem fo' hav' no feelings at all fo' de po' wooden foot man."

"Gahd! How yo' mean feelings? Wha' yo' want me fo' do? Hug yo' up?"

"Tek pity. . . ."

"Go 'way from heah I say. Don't come near me. Loose me befo' I go get de cutlass an' chop off yo' udder foot."

"Yo' know yo' won't do dat."

"Is dat so?"

"Yo' know yo' won't. . . ."

"Fo' true?"

"Yo' too kind. Yo' won't—yo' like me—"

"Oh, is dat de saht o' man yo' is, eh?"

"Wha' yo' mean? Tahlk, ooman, what saht o' man is dat?"

"T'ink dat ev'y ooman is de same. But yo' is a dam liar! Nutting can frighten me. All dem bag o' flour yo' 'a' got, an' dem silk shut, an' dem gold teets, an' dem Palama hats, yo' a spote round heah wid—dem don't frighten me. I is a woman what is usta t'ings. I got me hogs an' me fowls an' me potatoes. No wooden foot neygah man can frighten me wit' he clothes or he barrels o' cologne. . . ."

Yellow kerchief mopping his brow, he walked off . . . peg step, peg step . . . leaving Ella by the well, gazing with defiance in her being.

"What he t'ink I is, anyhow?"

"Go back an' lahn, go back an' lahn, dat not de way fi' cote."

The western sky of Barbadoes was ablaze. A mixture of fire and gold, it burned, and burned—into one vast sulphurous mass. It burned the houses, the trees, the windowpanes. The burnt glass did amazing color somersaults—turned brown and gold and lavender and red. It poured a burning liquid over the gap. It colored the water in the ponds a fierce dull yellowish gold. It flung on the corn and the peas and the star apples a lavender glow. It pitched its golden, flaming, iridescent shadow upon the lush of paw-paw and sunflower. It withered the petals of rose or sweet pea or violet or morning glory. Its flame upon the earth was mighty. Sunset over the gap paralyzed. Sunset shot weird amber tints in the eyes of the black peons . . . sent strange poetic dreams through the crinkly heads of mule boys tiredly bowed over the reins of some starved-out buckra cart horse.

Sunset at Ella's—"Go in yo' pen, sah, go in. . . ." Hogs, fowls, pigeons, geese, bastard creations, straggled waywardly in.

Smoke. Smoke is easy to smell. Ella quickly smelt it. Then she began to look for it. . . . Smoke and the sunset. A smoky sunset. No. The setting sun kept her from seeing it. But slowly it grew dim, dark; slowly the gold burned into a deep rich bronze . . . slowly it burned and burned . . . black.

"Somebody grass burnin'," Ella sniffed and looked about. The dense night helped. The smoke persisted. "Ah, dere it are." Ella paused, a hen, sick with the yaws, clutched to her bosom.

"Gahd, a cane fire." Vaults of black smoke rose. A winding, spouting pyramid of it. Black, greasy, caneless.

"It must be de church steeple, dem ministers is so careless. . . ." Ella watched, lured by the curving, spouting ascent.

"Miss Heath!" From the gap a voice called. "Fiah, Miss Heath, fiah, Poyah shop on fiah!" One of the Dalrimple children . . . speeding down the gap, to the rest of the folks. . . .

"Lahd, 'a' massie!"

The hen suddenly took flight out of Ella's arm, spilling the molasses and corn she had been feeding it. Emptying the bucket containing the relishes of her evening meal, she ran to the well and jerked it down it. Swiftly the bucket was jerked back up. Water splashed. It was a big bucket. With one grand sweep Ella swung it on her head. Ella was a mulatto, with plenty of soft black hair. She didn't need a cloth twisted and plaited to form a matting for her head. Her hair did that; it was thick enough. It could hold, balance a bucket.

The bucket sat on the crown of her head looking as if it had been created there. And Ella sailed on with it. She forgot to put out the fire under her food.

And down the gap she fled, the bucket of water on her head. Her strides were typical of the West Indian peasant woman—free, loose, firm. Zim zam, zim, zam. Her feet were made to traverse that stony gap. No stones defied her free, lithe approach. Left foot to right hand, right hand to left foot—and Ella swept down with amazing grace and ease. Her toes were broad; they encountered no obstacles. Her feet did not slip. The water did not splash. It was safe, firm, serene on top of her head.

Ella got in the broad road—easier. A sigh escaped her lips. The road was enlivened by one or two people coming up from town—

"Run, dahtah, the shop a bu'n."

"Quick, dem a need it."

It was dry; a little marl dust. Up the stony resilient incline she went, then swiftly down by the evergreen tree.

"Gahd, he is burnt out clean." All around the evergreen tree there used to be shadows. The fire sent gleams of firelight pelting through the dark. The shadows flew. You could have picked up a pin under the evergreen. . . .

Crowds of anxious hill dwellers gathered up the road. From Eagle Hall Corner a constable was coming with the white cork hat, the creaking shoes, the regal swagger of the black constabulary. . . .

It was easy for Ella to strain through the tiny crowd of folk up the embankment.

Fire singed Ella. Smoke dazed her, choked and repelled her. . . . "Go back dere, go back. You—stand back!"

"Where is Missah Poyah, where is Missah Poyah?" Ella screamed. A straw valise, label spattered—deckers' luggage—an old shirt—one or two stray sacks of split peas— the money canister.

Faces; old Bruin, "Where is Missah Poyah?" Ella pursued madly, collaring the weed gourmand. "Where is Missah Poyah?"

"Stand back!" the constable ordered, "stand back, and let 'em bring in de stretcher!"

Old Bruin gave way, talking loudly and excitedly. "He is in dey, yes, he is in dey . . . don't push me 'bout . . . I tell yo' he is in dey. Yo' must be drunk yo'self."

It was then that Ella realized how for nothing was her bucket of water.

The Yellow One

I

Once catching a glimpse of her, they swooped down like a brood of starving hawks. But it was the girl's first vision of the sea, and the superstitions of a Honduras peasant heritage tightened her grip on the old rusty canister she was dragging with a frantic effort on to the *Urubamba's* gangplank.

"Le' me help yo', dahtah," said one.

"Go 'way, man, yo' too farrad—'way!"

"'Im did got de fastiness fi' try fi' jump ahead o' me again, but mahn if yo' t'ink yo' gwine duh me outa a meal yo' is a dam pitty liar!"

"Wha' yo' ah try fi' do, leggo!" cried the girl, slapping the nearest one. But the shock of her words was enough to paralyze them.

They were a harum-scarum lot, hucksters, ex-cable divers and thugs of the coast, barefooted, brown-faced, raggedly—drifting from every cave and creek of the Spanish Main.

They withdrew, shocked, uncertain of their ears, staring at her; at her whom the peons of the lagoon idealized as *la madurita*: the yellow one.

Sensing the hostility, but unable to fathom it, she felt guilty of some untoward act, and guardedly lowered her eyes.

Flushed and hot, she seized the canister by the handle and started resuming the journey. It was heavy. More energy was required to move it than she had bargained on.

In the dilemma rescuing footsteps were heard coming down the gangplank. She was glad to admit she was stumped, and stood back, confronted by one of the crew. He was tall, some six feet and over, and a mestizo like herself. Latin blood bubbled in his veins, and it served at once to establish a ready means of communication between them.

"I'll take it," he said, quietly, "you go aboard—"

"Oh, many thanks," she said, "and do be careful, I've got the baby bottle in there and I wouldn't like to break it." All this in Spanish, a tongue spontaneously springing up between them.

She struggled up the gangplank, dodging a sling drooping tipsily on to the wharf. "Where are the passengers for Kingston station?" she asked.

"Yonder!" he pointed, speeding past her. Amongst a contortion of machinery, cargo, nets and hatch panels he deposited the trunk.

Gazing at his hardy hulk, two emotions seared her. She wanted to be grateful but he wasn't the sort of person she could offer a tip to. And he would readily see through her telling him that Alfred was down the dock changing the money.

But he warmed to her rescue. "Oh, that's alright," he said, quite illogically, "stay here till they close the hatch, then if I am not around, somebody will help you put it where you want it."

Noises beat upon her. Vendors of tropical fruits cluttered the wharf, kept up sensuous cries; stir and clamor and

screams rose from every corner of the ship. Men swerved
about her, the dock hands the crew, digging cargo off the pier
and spinning it into the yawning hatch.

"Wha' ah lot o' dem," she observed, "an' dem so black and
ugly. R—r—!" Her words had the anti-native quality of her
Jamaica spouse's, Alfred St. Xavier Mendez.

The hatch swelled, the bos'n closed it and the seige com-
menced. "If Ah did got any sense Ah would Ah wait till dem
clean way de rope befo' me mek de sailor boy put down de
trunk. How-somevah, de Lawd will provide, an' all me got fi'
do is put me trus' in Him till Halfred come."

With startling alacrity, her prayers were answered, for
there suddenly appeared a thin moonfaced decker, a coal-
black fellow with a red greasy scarf around his neck, his teeth
giddy with an ague he had caught in Puerta Tela and which
was destined never to leave him. He seized the trunk by one
end and helped her hoist it on the hatch. When he had finished, he didn't wait for her trepid words of thanks but flew
to the ship's rail, convulsively shaking.

She grew restive. "Wha' dat Halfred, dey, eh," she cried,
"wha' man can pacify time dough, eh?"

The stream of amassing deckers overran the *Urubamba*'s
decks. The din of parts being slugged to rights buzzed. An
oily strip of canvas screened the hatch. Deckers clamorously
crept underneath it.

The sea lay torpid, sizzling. Blue rust flaked off the
ship's sides shone upon it. It dazzled you. It was difficult to
divine its true color. Sometimes it was so blue it blinded you.
Another time it would turn with the cannon roar of the sun,
red. Nor was it the red of fire or of youth, of roses or of red

tulips. But a sullen, grizzled red. The red of a North Sea rover's icicled beard; the red of a red-headed woman's hair, the red of a red-hot oven. It gave to the water engulfing the ship a dark, copper-colored hue. It left on it jeweled crusts.

A bow-legged old Maroon, with a trunk on his head, explored the deck, smoking a gawky clay pipe of some fiery Jamaica bush and wailing, "Scout bway, scout bway, wha' yo' dey? De old man ah look fa' yo'." The trunk was beardy and fuzzy with the lashes of much-used rope. It was rapidly dusking, and a woman and an amazing brood of children came on. One pulled, screaming, at her skirt, one was astride a hip, another, an unclothed one, tugged enthusiastically at a full, ripened breast. A hoary old black man, in a long black coat, who had taken the Word, no doubt, to the yellow "heathen" of the fever-hot lagoon, shoeless, his hard white crash pants rolled up above his hairy, veiny calves, with a lone yellow pineapple as his sole earthly reward.

A tar-black Jamaica sister, in a gown of some noisy West Indian silk, her face entirely removed by the shadowy girth of a leghorn hat, waltzed grandly up on the deck. The edge of her skirt in one hand, after the manner of the ladies at Wimbledon, in the other a fluttering macaw, she was twittering, "Hawfissah, hawfissah, wear is de hawfissah, he?" Among the battering hordes there were less brusque folk; a native girl—a flower, a brown flower—was alone, rejecting the opulent offer of bunk, quietly vowing to pass two nights of sleepful concern until she got to Santiago. And two Costa Rica maidens, white, dainty, resentful and uncommunicative.

He came swaggering at last. La Madurita said "Wha' yo' been, Halfred, all dis lang time, no?"

"Cho, it wuz de man dem down dey," he replied, "dem keep me back." He gave her the sleeping child, and slipped down to doze on the narrow hatch.

In a mood of selfless bluster he was returning to Kingston. He adored Jamaica. He would go on sprees of work and daring, to the jungles of Changuinola or the Cut at Culebra, but such flights, whether for a duration of one or ten years, were uplifted mainly by the traditional deprivations of Hindu coolies or Polish immigrants—sunless, joyless. Similarly up in Cabello; work, sleep, work; day in and day out for six forest-hewing years. And on Sabbaths a Kentucky evangelist, a red-headed hypochondriac, the murky hue of a British buckra from the beat of the tropic sun, tearfully urged the blacks to embrace the teachings of the Lord Jesus Christ before the wrath of Satan engulfed them. Then, one day, on a tramp to Salamanca, a fancy struck him. It stung, was unexpected. He was unused to the sensations it set going. It related to a vision—something he had surreptitiously encountered. Behind a planter's hut he had seen it. He was slowly walking along the street, shaded by a row of plum trees, and there she was, gloriously unaware of him, bathing her feet in ample view of the sky. She was lovely to behold. Her skin was the ripe red gold of the Honduras half-breed. It sent the blood streaming to his head. He paused and wiped the sweat from his face. He looked at her, calculating. Five—six—seven-fifty. Yes, that'd do. With seven hundred and fifty pounds, he'd dazzle the foxy folk of Kingston with the mellow *Spanish* beauty of her.

In due time, and by ample means, he had been able to bring round the girl's hitherto *chumbo*-hating folk.

"Him mus' be hungry," she said, gazing intently at the baby's face.

"Cho," replied Alfred, "leave de picknee alone, le' de gal picknee sleep." He rolled over, face downwards, and folded his arms under his chin. He wore a dirty khaki shirt, made in the States, dark green corduroy pants and big yellow shoes which he seldom took off.

Upright on the trunk, the woman rocked the baby and nursed it. By this time the hatch was overcrowded with deckers.

Down on the dock, oxen were yoked behind wagons of crated bananas. Gnawing on plugs of hard black tobacco and firing reels of spit to every side of them, New Orleans "crackers" swearingly cursed the leisurely lack of native labor. Scaly ragamuffins darted after boxes of stale cheese and crates of sun-sopped iced apples that were dumped in the sea.

II

The dawning sunlight pricked the tarpaulin and fell upon the woman's tired, sleep-sapped face. Enamel clanged and crashed. A sickly, sour-sweet odor pervaded the hatch. The sea was calm, gulls scuttled low, seizing and ecstatically devouring some reckless, sky-drunk sprat.

"Go, no, Halfred," cried the woman, the baby in her arms, "an' beg de backra man fi' giv' yo' a can o' hot water fi' mek de baby tea. Go no?"

He rolled over lazily; his loggish yellow bulk solid, dispirited. "Cho, de man dem no ha' no hot water, giv' she a lemon, no, she na'h cry." He tossed back again, his chin on his arms, gazing at the glorious procession of the sun.

"Even de man dem, ovah yondah," she cried gesticulating, "a hold a kangfarance fi' get some hot water. Why yo' don't get up an' go, no man? Me can't handastan' yo', sah."

A conspiration, a pandemonium threatened—the deckers.

"How de bleedy hell dem heckspeck a man fi' trabble tree days an' tree whole a nights beout giv' him any hot watah fi' mek even a can o' tea is somet'ing de hagent at Kingston gwine hav' fi' pint out to me w'en de boat dey lan'—"

"Hey, mistah hawfissah, yo' got any hot watah?

"Hot watah, mistah?"

"Me will giv' yo' a half pint o' red rum if yo' giv' me a quatty wut' o' hot watah."

"Come, no, man, go get de watah, no?"

"Ripe apples mek me t'row up!"

"Green tamarin' mek me tummack sick!"

"Sahft banana mek me fainty!"

"Fish sweetie giv' me de dysentery."

Craving luscious Havana nights the ship's scullions hid in refuse cans or in grub for the Chinks hot water which they peddled to the miserable deckers.

"Get up, no Halfred, an' go buy some o' de watah," the girl cried, "de baby a cry."

Of late he didn't answer her any more. And it was useless to depend upon him. Frantic at the baby's pawing of the clotted air, at the cold dribbling from its twisted mouth, which turned down a trifle at the ends like Alfred's, she began conjecturing on the use to which a decker could put a cup of the precious liquid. Into it one might pour a gill of goat's milk—a Cuban *señora*, a decker of several voyages, had fortified herself with a bucket of it—or melt a sprig of peppermint or a lump of clove or a root of ginger. So many tropical things one could do with a cup of hot water.

The child took on the color of its sweltering environs. It refused to be pacified by sugared words. It was hungry and it wished to eat, to feel coursing down its throat something warm and delicious. It kicked out of its mother's hand the toy engine she locomotioned before it. It cried, it ripped with its naked toes a hole in her blouse. It kept up an irrepressible racket.

The child's agony drove her to reckless alternatives. "If you don't go, then I'll go, yo' lazy t'ing," she said, depositing the baby beside him and disappearing down the galley corridor.

Her bare earth-red feet slid on the hot, sizzling deck. The heat came roaring at her. It swirled enveloping her. It was a dingy corridor and there were pigmy paneled doors every inch along it. It wasn't clear to her whither she was bound; the vaporing heat dizzied things. But the scent of stewing meat and vegetables lured her on. It sent her scudding in and out of barrels of cold storage, mounds of ash debris of an exotic kind. It shot her into dark twining circles of men, talking. They either paused or grew lecherous at her approach. Some of the doors to the crew's quarters were open and as she passed white men'd stick out their heads and call, pull, tug at her. Grimy ash-stained faces; leprous, flesh-crazed hands. Onward she fled, into the roaring, fuming galley.

Heat. Hearths aglow. Stoves aglow. Dishes clattering. Engines, donkey-engines, wheezing. Bright-faced and flame-haired Swedes and Bristol cockneys cursing. Half-nude figures of bronze and crimson shouting, spearing, mending the noisy fire. The wet, clean, brick-colored deck danced to the

rhythm of the ship. Darky waiters—white shirt bosoms—
black bow ties—black, braided uniforms—spat entire menus
at the blond cooks.

"Slap it on dey, Dutch, don't starve de man."

"Hey, Hubigon, tightenin' up on any mo' hoss flesh
to-day?"

"Come on fellahs, let's go—"

"There's my boy Porto Rico again Hubigon, Ah tell yo'
he is a sheik, tryin' to git nex' to dat hot yallah mama."

On entering she had turned, agonized and confused, to a
lone yellow figure by the port hole.

"Oh, it's you," she exclaimed, and smiled wanly.

He was sourly sweeping dishes, forks, egg-stained things
into a mossy wooden basket which he hoisted and dropped
into a cesspool of puttering water.

He paused, blinking uncomprehendingly.

"You," she was catching at mementoes, "you remember—
you helped me—my trunk—"

"Oh, yes, I remember," he said slowly. He was Cuban,
mix-blooded, soft-haired, and to him, as she stood there, a
bare, primitive soul, her beauty and her sex seemed to be in
utmost contrast to his mechanical surroundings.

"Can you," she said, in that half-hesitant way of hers "give
me some hot watah fo' my baby?"

He was briefly attired; overalls, a dirty, pink singlet. His
reddish-yellow face, chest and neck shone with the grease
and sweat. His face was buttered with it.

"Sure," he replied, seizing an empty date can on the ledge
of the port hole and filling it. "Be careful," he cautioned,
handing it back to her.

She took it and their eyes meeting, fell.

She started to go, but a burning touch of his hand possessed her.

"Wait," he said, "I almost forgot something." From beneath the machine he exhumed an old moist gold dust box. Inside it he had pummeled, by some ornate instinct, odds and ends—echoes of the breakfast table. He gave the box to her, saying, "If any one should ask you where you got it, just say Jota Arosemena gave it to you."

"Hey, Porto Rico, wha' the hell yo' git dat stuff at, hotting stuff fo' decks?"

Both of them turned, and the Cuban paled at the jaunty mug of the cook's Negro mate.

"You speak to me?" he said, ice cool.

Hate shone on the black boy's face. "Yo' heard me!" he growled. "Yo' ain't cock-eyed." Ugly, grim, black, his face wore an uneasy leer. He was squat and bleary-eyed.

A son of the Florida Gulf, he hated "Porto Rico" for reasons planted deep in the Latin's past. He envied him the gentle texture of his hair. On mornings in the galley where they both did the toilet he would poke fun at the Cuban's meticulous care in parting it. "Yo' ain't gwine sho," Hubigon'd growl. "Yo' don't have to dress up like no lady man." And Jota, failing to comprehend the point of view, would question, "What's the matter with you, mang, you mek too much noise, mang." Hubigon despised him because he was yellow-skinned; one night in Havana he had spied him and the chef cook, a nifty, freckle-faced Carolina "cracker" for whom the cook's mate had no earthly use, and the baker's assistant, a New Orleans creole—although the Negro waiters abroad were sure he was a "yallah" nigger—drinking *anee* in a high hat café on the prado which barred jet-black American Negroes. He loathed the Latin for his good looks and once at a port on the Buenaventura River they had gone ashore and met two native girls. One was white, her lips pure as the petals of a water lily; the other was a flaming mulatto. That night, on the steps of an adobe hut, a great, low moon in the sky, both forgot the presence of the cook's mate and pledged tearstained love to Jota. "An' me standin' right by him, doin' fadeaway." He envied Jota his Cuban nationality for over and over again he had observed that the Latin was the nearest thing to a white man the *ofay* men aboard had yet met. They'd play cards with him—something they never did with the Negro crew—they'd gang with him in foreign ports, they'd listen in a "natural" sort of way to all the bosh he had to say.

Now all the mate's pent-up wrath came foaming to the front.

He came up, the girl having tarried, a cocky, chesty air about him. He made deft, telling jabs at the vapors enmeshing him. "Yo' can't do that," he said, indicating the victuals, "like hell yo' kin! Who de hell yo' t'ink yo' is anyhow? Yo' ain't bettah'n nobody else. Put it back, big boy, befo' Ah starts whisperin' to de man. Wha' yo' t'ink yo' is at, anyhow, in Porto Rico, where yo' come fum at? Com' handin' out poke chops an' cawn muffins, like yo' is any steward. Yo' cain't do dat, ole man."

It slowly entered the other's brain—all this edgy, snappy, darky talk. But the essence of it was aggressively reflected in the mate's behavior. Hubigon made slow measured steps forward, and the men came flocking to the corner.

"Go to it, Silver King, step on his corns."

"Stick him with a ice pick!"

"Easy fellahs, the steward's comin'."

All of them suddenly fell away. The steward, initiating some fruit baron into the mysteries of the galley, came through, giving them time to speed back to their posts unobserved. The tension subsided, and Jota once more fed the hardware to the dish machine.

As she flew through the corridor all sorts of faces, white ones, black ones, brown ones, leered sensually at her. Like tongues of flame, hands sped after her. Her steps quickened, her heart beat faster and faster till she left behind her the droning of the galley, and safely ascending the hatch, felt on her face the soft, cool breezes of the Caribbean ocean.

Alfred was sitting up, the unpacified baby in his arms.

"'Im cry all de time yo' went 'way," he said, "wha' yo' t'ink is de mattah wit' 'im, he? Yo' t'ink him tummack a hut 'im?"

"Him is hungry, dat is wha' is de mattah wit' 'im! Move, man! 'Fo Ah knock yo', yah! Giv' me 'im, an' get outa me way! Yo' is only a dyam noosant!"

"Well, what is de mattah, now?" he cried in unfeigned surprise.

"Stid o' gwine fo' de watah yo'self yo' tan' back yah an' giv' hawdahs an' worryin' wha' is de mattah wit' de picknee."

"Cho, keep quiet, woman, an' le' me lie down." Satisfied, he rolled back on the hatch, fatuously staring at the sun sweeping the tropic blue sea.

"T'un ovah, Halfred, an' lif' yo' big able self awf de baby, yo' Ah crush 'im to debt," she said, awake at last. The baby was awake and ravenous before dawn and refused to be quieted by the witty protestations of the Jamaica laborers scrubbing down the deck. But it was only after the sun, stealing a passage through a crack in the canvas, had warmed a spot on the girl's mouth, that she was constrained to respond to his zestful rantings. "Hey, yo' heah de picknee ah bawl all de time an' yo' won't even tek heed—move yah man!" She thrust the sleeping leg aside and drawing the child to her, stuck a breast in his mouth.

The boat had encountered a sultry sea, and was dipping badly. Water flooded her decks. Getting wet, dozing deckers crawled higher on top of each other. The sea was blue as indigo and white reels of foam swirled past as the ship dove ahead.

It was a disgusting spectacle. There was the sea, drumming on the tinsel sides of the ship, and on top of the terror thus resulting rose a wretched wail from the hatch, "Watah! Hot Watah!"

The galley was the Bastille. Questioning none, the Yellow One, giving the baby to Alfred rushed to the door, and flung herself through it. Once in the corridor, the energy of a dynamo possessed her. Heated mist drenched her. She slid on grimy, sticky deck.

He was hanging up the rag on a brace of iron over the port hole. His jaws were firm, grim, together.

The rest of the galley was a foetic blur to her.

He swung around, and his restless eyes met her. He was for the moment paralyzed. His eyes bore into hers. He itched to toss at her words, words, words! He wanted to say, "Oh, why couldn't you stay away—ashore—down there—at the end of the world—anywhere but on this ship."

"Some water," she said with that gentle half-hesitant

smile of hers, "can I get some hot water for my little baby?" And she extended the skillet.

He took it to the sink, his eyes still on hers. The water rained into it like bullets and he brought it to her.

But a sound polluted the lovely quiet.

"Hey, Porto Rico, snap into it! Dis ain't no time to get foolin' wit' no monkey jane. Get a move on dey, fellah, an' fill dis pail full o' water."

He was sober, afar, as he swept a pale, tortured face at Hubigon. As if it were the song of a lark, he swung back to the girl, murmuring, "Ah, but you didn't tell me," he said, "you didn't tell me what the baby is, a boy or girl?" For answer, the girl's eyes widened in terror at something slowly forming behind him.

But it was not without a shadow, and Jota swiftly ducked. The mallet went galloping under the machine. He rose and faced the cook's mate. But Hubigon was not near enough to objectify the jab, sent as fast as the fangs of a striking snake, and Jota fell, cursing, to the hushed cries of the woman. For secretly easing over to the fireplace Hubigon had taken advantage of the opening to grasp a spear and as the other was about to rise brought it thundering down on the tip of his left shoulder. It sent him thudding to the deck in a pool of claret. The cook's mate, his red, red tongue licking his mouth after the manner of a collie in from a strenuous run, pounced on the emaciated figure in the corner, and kicked and kicked it murderously. He kicked him in the head, in the mouth, in the ribs. When he struggled to rise, he sent him back to the floor, dizzy from short, telling jabs with the tip of his boot.

Pale, impassive, the men were prone to take sides. Unconsciously forming a ring, the line was kept taut. Sometimes it surged; once an Atlanta mulatto had to wrest a fiery spear from Foot Works, Hubigon's side kick, and thrust it back in its place. "Keep outa this, if you don't want to get your goddam head mashed in," he said. A woman, a crystal panel in the gray, ugly pattern, tore, fought, had to be kept sane by raw, meaty hands.

Gasping, Hubigon stood by, his eyes shining at the other's languid effort to rise. "Stan' back, fellahs, an' don't interfere. Let 'im come!" With one shoulder jaunty and a jaw risen, claret-drenched, redolent of the stench and grime of Hubigon's boot, parts of it clinging to him, the Cuban rose. A cruel scowl was on his face.

The crowd stood back, and there was sufficient room for them. Hubigon was ripping off his shirt, and licking his red, bleeding lips. He circled the ring like a snarling jungle beast. "Hol' at fuh me, Foot Works, I'm gwine sho' dis monkey wheh he get off at." He was dancing round, jabbing, tapping at ghosts, awaiting the other's beastly pleasure.

As one cowed he came, his jaw swollen. Then with the vigor of a maniac he straightened, facing the mate. He shot out his left. It had the wings of a dart and juggled the mate on the chin. Hubigon's ears tingled distantly. For the particle of a second he was groggy, and the Cuban moored in with the right, flush on the chin. Down the cook's mate went. Leaping like a tiger cat, Jota was upon him, burying his claws in the other's bared, palpitating throat. His eyes gleamed like a tiger cat's. He held him by the throat and squeezed him till his tongue came out. He racked him till the blood seeped through his ears. Then, in a frenzy of frustration, he lifted him up, and pounded with his head on the bared deck. He pounded till the shirt on his back split into ribbons.

"Jesus, take him awf o' him—he's white orready."

"Now, boys, this won't do," cried the baker, a family man. "Come."

And some half dozen of them, running counter to the traditions of the coast, ventured to slug them apart. It was a gruesome job, and Hubigon, once freed, his head and chest smeared with blood, black, was ready to peg at a lancing La Barrie snake.

In the scuffle the woman collapsed, fell under the feet of the milling crew.

"Here," some one cried, "take hold o' her, Butch, she's your kind—she's a decker—hatch four—call the doctor somebody, will ya?"

They took her on a stretcher to the surgeon's room.

The sun had leaped ahead. A sizzling luminosity drenched the sea. Aft the deckers were singing hosannas to Jesus and preparing to walk the gorgeous earth.

Only Alfred St. Xavier Mendez was standing with the baby in his arms, now on its third hunger-nap, gazing with a bewildered look at the deserted door to the gallery. "Me wondah wha' mek she 'tan' so lang," he whispered anxiously.

Imperceptibly shedding their drapery of mist, there rose above the prow of the *Urubamba* the dead blue hills of Jamaica.

The Wharf Rats

I

Among the motley crew recruited to dig the Panama Canal were artisans from the four ends of the earth. Down in the Cut drifted hordes of Italians, Greeks, Chinese, Negroes—a hardy, sun-defying set of white, black and yellow men. But the bulk of the actual brawn for the work was supplied by the dusky peons of those coral isles in the Caribbean ruled by Britain, France and Holland.

At the Atlantic end of the Canal the blacks were herded in boxcar huts buried in the jungles of "Silver City"; in the murky tenements perilously poised on the narrow banks of Faulke's River; in the low, smelting cabins of Coco Té. The "Silver Quarters" harbored the inky ones, their wives and pickaninnies.

As it grew dark the hewers at the Ditch, exhausted, half-asleep, naked but for wormy singlets, would hum queer creole tunes, play on guitar or piccolo, and jig to the rhythm of the *coombia*. It was a *brujerial* chant, for *obeah*, a heritage of the French colonial, honeycombed the life of the Negro laboring camps. Over smoking pots, on black, death-black nights legends of the bloodiest were recited till they became the essence of a sort of Negro Koran. One refuted them at

the price of one's breath. And to question the verity of the
obeah, to dismiss or reject it as the ungodly rite of some lurid,
crack-brained Islander was to be an accursed pale-face, dog of
a white. And the *obeah* man, in a fury of rage, would throw a
machete at the heretic's head or—worse—burn on his door-
step at night a pyre of Maubé bark or green Ganja weed.

On the banks of a river beyond Cristobal, Coco Té
sheltered a colony of Negroes enslaved to the *obeah*. Near a
roundhouse, daubed with smoke and coal ash, a river serenely
flowed away and into the guava region, at the eastern tip of
Monkey Hill. Across the bay from it was a sand bank—a rising out of the sea—where ships stopped for coal.

In the first of the six chinky cabins making up the family
quarters of Coco Té lived a stout, potbellied St. Lucian, black
as the coal hills he mended, by the name of Jean Baptiste.
Like a host of the native St. Lucian emigrants, Jean Baptiste
forgot where the French in him ended and the English began.
His speech was the petulant *patois* of the unlettered French
black. Still, whenever he lapsed into His Majesty's English, it
was with a thick Barbadian bias.

A coal passer at the Dry Dock, Jean Baptiste was a man
of intense piety. After work, by the glow of a red, setting sun,
he would discard his crusted overalls, get in starched *crocus
bag*, aping the Yankee foreman on the other side of the track
in the "Gold Quarters," and loll on his coffee-vined porch.
There, dozing in a bamboo rocker, Celestin, his second wife,
a becomingly stout brown beauty from Martinique, chanted
gospel hymns to him.

Three sturdy sons Jean Baptiste's first wife had borne
him—Philip, the eldest, a good-looking, black fellow; Ernest,

shifty, cunning; and Sandel, aged eight. Another boy, said to be wayward and something of a ne'er-do-well, was sometimes spoken of. But Baptiste, a proud, disdainful man, never once referred to him in the presence of his children. No vagabond son of his could eat from his table or sit at his feet unless he went to "meeting." In brief, Jean Baptiste was a religious man. It was a thrust at the omnipresent *obeah*. He went to "meeting." He made the boys go, too. All hands went, not to the Catholic Church, where Celestin secretly worshiped, but to the English Plymouth Brethren in the Spanish city of Colon.

Stalking about like a ghost in Jean Baptiste's household was a girl, a black ominous Trinidad girl. Had Jean Baptiste been a man given to curiosity about the nature of women, he would have viewed skeptically Maffi's adoption by Celestin. But Jean Baptiste was a man of lofty unconcern, and so Maffi remained there, shadowy, obdurate.

And Maffi was such a hardworking *patois* girl. From the break of day she'd be at the sink, brightening the tinware. It was she who did the chores which Madame congenitally shirked. And towards sundown, when the labor trains had emptied, it was she who scoured the beach for cockles for Jean Baptiste's epicurean palate.

And as night fell, Maffi, a long, black figure, would disappear in the dark to dream on top of a canoe hauled up on the mooning beach. An eternity Maffi'd sprawl there, gazing at the frosting of the stars and the glitter of the black sea.

A cabin away lived a family of Tortola mulattoes by the name of Boyce. The father was also a man who piously went to "meeting"—gaunt and hollow-cheeked. The eldest boy, Esau, had been a journeyman tailor for ten years; the girl next him, Ora, was plump, dark, freckled; others came—a string of ulcered girls until finally a pretty, opaque one, Maura.

Of the Bantu tribe Maura would have been a person to turn and stare at. Crossing the line into Cristobal or Colon—a city of rarefied gayety—she was often mistaken for a native *señorita* or an urbanized Cholo Indian girl. Her skin was the reddish yellow of old gold and in her eyes there lurked the glint of mother-of-pearl. Her hair, long as a jungle elf's was jettish, untethered. And her teeth were whiter than the full-blooded black Philip's.

Maura was brought up, like the children of Jean Baptiste, in the Plymouth Brethren. But the Plymouth Brethren was a harsh faith to bring hemmed-in peasant children up in, and Maura, besides, was of a gentle romantic nature. Going to the Yankee commissary at the bottom of Eleventh and Front Streets, she usually wore a leghorn hat. With flowers bedecking it, she'd look in it older, much older than she really was. Which was an impression quite flattering to her. For Maura, unknown to Philip, was in love—in love with San Tie, a Chinese half-breed, son of a wealthy canteen proprietor in Colon. But San Tie liked to go fishing and deer hunting up the Monkey Hill lagoon, and the object of his occasional visits to Coco Té was the eldest son of Jean Baptiste. And thus it was through Philip that Maura kept in touch with the young Chinese Maroon.

One afternoon Maura, at her wits' end flew to the shed roof to Jean Baptiste's kitchen.

"Maffi," she cried, the words smoky on her lips, "Maffi, when Philip come in to-night tell 'im I want fo' see 'im particular, yes?"

"*Sacre gache!* All de time Philip, Philip!" growled the Trinidad girl, as Maura, in heartaching preoccupation, sped towards the lawn. "Why she no le' 'im alone, yes?" And with a spatter she flecked the hunk of lard on Jean Baptiste's stewing okras.

As the others filed up front after dinner that evening Maffi said to Philip, pointing to the cabin across the way, "She—she want fo' see yo'."

Instantly Philip's eyes widened. Ah, he had good news for Maura! San Tie, after an absence of six days, was coming to Coco Té Saturday to hunt on the lagoon. And he'd relish the joy that'd flood Maura's face as she glimpsed the idol of her heart, the hero of her dreams! And Philip, a true son of Jean Baptiste, loved to see others happy, ecstatic.

But Maffi's curious rumination checked him. "All de time, Maura, Maura, me can't understand it, yes. But no mind, me go stop it, *oui*, me go stop it, so help me—"

He crept up to her, gently holding her by the shoulders.

"Le' me go, *sacre!*" She shook off his hands bitterly. "Le' me go—yo' go to yo' Maura." And she fled to her room, locking the door behind her.

Philip sighed. He was a generous, good-natured sort. But it was silly to try to enlighten Maffi. It wasn't any use. He could as well have spoken to the tattered torsos the lazy waves puffed up on the shores of Coco Té.

II

"Philip, come on, a ship is in—let's go." Ernest, the wharf rat, seized him by the arm.

"Come," he said, "let's go before it's too late. I want to get some money, yes."

Dashing out of the house the two boys made for the wharf. It was dusk. Already the Hindus in the bachelor quarters were mixing their *rotie* and the Negroes in their singlets were smoking and cooling off. Night was rapidly approaching. Sunset, an iridescent bit of molten gold, was enriching the stream with its last faint radiance.

The boys stole across the lawn and made their way to the pier.

"Careful," cried Philip, as Ernest slid between a prong of oyster-crusted piles to a raft below, "careful, these shells cut wussah'n a knife."

On the raft the boys untied a rowboat they kept stowed away under the dock, got into it and pushed off. The liner still had two hours to dock. Tourists crowded its decks. Veering away from the barnacled piles the boys eased out into the churning ocean.

It was dusk. Night would soon be upon them. Philip took the oars while Ernest stripped down to loin cloth.

"Come, Philip, let me paddle—" Ernest took the oars. Afar on the dusky sea a whistle echoed. It was the pilot's signal to the captain of port. The ship would soon dock.

The passengers on deck glimpsed the boys. It piqued their curiosity to see two black boys in a boat amid stream.

"All right, mistah," cried Ernest, "a penny, mistah."

He sprang at the guilder as it twisted and turned through a streak of silver dust to the bottom of the sea. Only the tips of his crimson toes—a sherbet-like foam—and up he came with the coin between his teeth.

Deep sea gamin, Philip off yonder, his mouth noisy with coppers, gargled, "This way, sah, as far as yo' like, mistah."

An old red-bearded Scot, in spats and mufti, presumably a lover of the exotic in sport, held aloft a sovereign. A sovereign! Already red, and sore by virtue of the leaps and plunges in the briny swirl, Philip's eyes bulged at its yellow gleam.

"Ovah yah, sah—"

Off in a whirlpool the man tossed it. And like a garfish Philip took after it, a falling arrow in the stream. His body, once in the water, tore ahead. For a spell the crowd on the ship held its breath. "Where is he?" "Where is the nigger swimmer gone to?" Even Ernest, driven to the boat by the race for such an ornate prize, cold, shivering, his teeth chattering—even he watched with trembling and anxiety. But Ernest's concern was of a deeper kind. For there, where Philip had leaped, was Deathpool—a spawning place for sharks, for barracudas!

But Philip rose—a brief gurgling sputter—a ripple on the sea—and the Negro's crinkled head was above the water.

"Hey!" shouted Ernest, "there, Philip! Down!"

And down Philip plunged. One—two—minutes. God, how long they seemed! And Ernest anxiously waited. But the bubble on the water boiled, kept on boiling—a sign that life still lasted! It comforted Ernest.

Suddenly Philip, panting, spitting, pawing, dashed through the water like a streak of lightning.

"Shark!" cried a voice aboard ship. "Shark! There he is, a great big one! Run, boy! Run for your life!"

From the edge of the boat Philip saw the monster as

twice, thrice it circled the boat. Several times the shark made
a dash for it endeavoring to strike it with its murderous tail.

The boys quietly made off. But the shark still followed
the boat. It was a pale-green monster. In the glittering dusk
it seemed black to Philip. Fattened on the swill of the abattoir nearby and the beef tossed from the decks of countless
ships in port it had become used to the taste of flesh and the
smell of blood.

"Yo' know, Ernest," said Philip, as he made the boat fast
to a raft, "one time I thought he wuz rubbin' 'gainst me belly.
He wuz such a big able one. But it wuz wuth it, Ernie, it wuz
wuth it—"

In his palm there was a flicker of gold. Ernest emptied
his loin cloth and together they counted the money, dressed
and trudged back to the cabin.

On the lawn Philip met Maura. Ernest tipped his cap,
left his brother, and went into the house. As he entered
Maffi, pretending to be scouring a pan, was flushed and mute
as a statue. And Ernest, starved, went in the dining room
and for a long time stayed there. Unable to bear it any longer,
Maffi sang out, "Ernest, whey Philip dey?"

"Outside—some whey—ah talk to Maura—"

"Yo' sure yo' no lie, Ernest?" she asked, suspended.

"Yes, up cose, I jes' lef' 'im 'tandin' out dey—why?"

"Nutton—"

He suspected nothing. He went on eating while Maffi
tiptoed to the shed roof. Yes, confound it, there he was, near
the stand-pipe, talking to Maura!

"Go stop *ee, oui*," she hissed impishly. "Go 'top ee, yes."

III

Low, shadowy, the sky painted Maura's face bronze. The sea, noisy, enraged, sent a blob of wind about her black, wavy hair. And with her back to the sea, her hair blew loosely about her face.

"D'ye think, d'ye think he really likes me, Philip?"

"I'm positive he do, Maura," vowed the youth.

And an ageing faith shone in Maura's eyes. No longer was she a silly, insipid girl. Something holy, reverent had touched her. And in so doing it could not fail to leave an impress of beauty. It was worshipful. And it mellowed, ripened her.

Weeks she had waited for word of San Tie. And the springs of Maura's life took on a noble ecstasy. Late at night, after the others had retired, she'd sit up in bed, dreaming. Sometimes they were dreams of envy. For Mama began to look with eyes of comparison upon the happiness of the Italian wife of the boss riveter at the Dry Dock—the lady on the other side of the railroad tracks in the "Gold Quarters" for whom she sewed—who got a fresh baby every year and who danced in a world of silks and satins. Yes, Maura had dreams, love dreams of San Tie, the flashy half-breed, son of a Chinese beer seller and a Jamaica Maroon, who had swept her off her feet by a playful wink of the eye.

"Tell me, Philip, does he work? Or does he play the lottery—what does he do, tell me!"

"I dunno," Philip replied with mock lassitude, "I dunno myself—"

"But it doesn't matter, Philip. I don't want to be nosy, see? I'm simply curious about everything that concerns him, see?"

Ah, but Philip wished to cherish Maura, to shield her, be kind to her. And so he lied to her. He did not tell her he had first met San Tie behind the counter of his father's saloon in the Colon tenderloin, for he would have had to tell, besides, why he, Philip, had gone there. And that would have led him, a youth of meager guile, to Celestin Baptiste's mulish regard for anisette which he procured her. He dared not tell her, well-meaning fellow that he was, what San Tie, a fiery comet in the night life of the district, had said to him the day before. "She sick in de head, yes," he had said. "Ah, me no dat saht o' man—don't she know no bettah, egh, Philip?" But Philip desired to be kindly, and hid it from Maura.

"What is to-day?" she cogitated, aloud, "Tuesday. You say he's comin' fo' hunt Saturday, Philip? Wednesday—four more days. I can wait. I can wait. I'd wait a million years fo' 'im, Philip."

But Saturday came and Maura, very properly, was shy as a duck. Other girls, like Hilda Long, a Jamaica brunette, the flower of a bawdy cabin up by the abattoir, would have been less genteel. Hilda would have caught San Tie by the lapels of his coat and in no time would have got him told.

But Maura was lowly, trepid, shy. To her he was a dream—a luxury to be distantly enjoyed. He was not to be touched. And she'd wait till he decided to come to her. And there was no fear, either, of his ever failing to come. Philip had seen to that. Had not he been the intermediary between them? And all Maura needed now was to sit back, and wait till San Tie came to her.

And besides, who knows, brooded Maura, San Tie might be a bashful fellow.

But when, after an exciting hunt, the Chinese mulatto returned from the lagoon, nodded stiffly to her, said good-by to Philip and kept on to the scarlet city, Maura was frantic.

"Maffi," she said, "tell Philip to come here quick—"

It was the same as touching a match to the *patois* girl's dynamite. "Yo' mek me sick," she said. "Go call he yo'self, yo' ole hag, yo' ole fire hag yo'." But Maura, flighty in despair, had gone on past the lawn.

"Ah go stop *ee, oui*," she muttered diabolically, "Ah go stop it, yes. This very night."

Soon as she got through lathering the dishes she tidied up and came out on the front porch.

It was a humid dusk, and the glowering sky sent a species of fly—bloody as a tick—buzzing about Jean Baptiste's porch. There he sat, rotund, and sleepy-eyed, rocking and languidly brushing the darting imps away.

"Wha' yo' gwine, Maffi?" asked Celestin Baptiste, fearing to wake the old man.

"Ovah to de Jahn Chinaman shop, mum," answered Maffi unheeding.

"Fi' what?"

"Fi' buy some wash blue, mum."

And she kept on down the road past the Hindu kiosk to the Negro mess house.

IV

"Oh, Philip," cried Maura, "I am so unhappy. Didn't he ask about me at all? Didn't he say he'd like to visit me—didn't he giv' yo' any message fo' me, Philip?"

The boy toyed with a blade of grass. His eyes were downcast. Sighing heavily he at last spoke. "No, Maura, he didn't ask about you."

"What, he didn't ask about me? Philip? I don't believe it! Oh, my God!"

She clung to Philip, mutely; her face, her breath coming warm and fast.

"I wish to God I'd never seen either of you," cried Philip.

"Ah, but wasn't he your friend, Philip? Didn't yo' tell me that?" And the boy bowed his head sadly.

"Answer me!" she screamed, shaking him. "Weren't you his friend?"

"Yes, Maura—"

"But you lied to me, Philip, you lied to me! You took messages from me—you brought back—lies!" Two *pearls*, large as pigeon's eggs, shone in Maura's burnished face.

"To think," she cried in a hollow sepulchral voice, "that I dreamed about a ghost, a man who didn't exist. Oh, God, why should I suffer like this? Why was I ever born? What did I do, what did my people do, to deserve such misery as this?"

She rose, leaving Philip with his head buried in his hands. She went into the night, tearing her hair, scratching her face, raving.

"Oh, how happy I was! I was a happy girl! I was so young and I had such merry dreams! And I wanted so little! I was carefree—"

Down to the shore of the sea she staggered, the wind behind her, the night obscuring her.

"Maura!" cried Philip, running after her. "Maura! come back!"

Great sheaves of clouds buried the moon, and the wind bearing up from the sea bowed the cypress and palm lining the beach.

"Maura—Maura—"

He bumped into some one, a girl, black, part of the dense pattern of the tropical night.

"Maffi," cried Philip, "Have you seen Maura down yondah?"

The girl quietly stared at him. Had Philip lost his mind?

"Talk, no!" he cried, exasperated.

And his quick tones sharpened Maffi's vocal anger. Thrusting him aside, she thundered, "Think I'm she keeper! Go'n look fo' she yo'self. I is not she keeper! Le' me pass, move!"

Towards the end of the track he found Maura, heart-rendingly weeping.

"Oh, don't cry, Maura! Never mind, Maura!"

He helped her to her feet, took her to the stand-pipe on the lawn, bathed her temples and sat soothingly, uninterruptingly, beside her.

V

At daybreak the next morning Ernest rose and woke Philip.

He yawned, put on the loin cloth, seized a "cracked licker" skillet and stole cautiously out of the house. Of late Jean Baptiste had put his foot down on his sons' copper-diving proclivities. And he kept at the head of his bed a greased cat-o'-nine-tails which he would use on Philip himself if the occasion warranted.

"Come on, Philip, let's go—"

Yawning and scratching Philip followed. The grass on the lawn was bright and icy with the dew. On the railroad tracks the six o'clock labor trains were coupling. A rosy mist flooded the dawn. Out in the stream the tug *Exotic* snorted in a heavy fog.

On the wharf Philip led the way to the rafts below.

"Look out fo' that *crapeau*, Ernest, don't step on him, he'll spit on you."

The frog splashed into the water. Prickle-backed crabs and oysters and myriad other shells spawned on the rotting piles. The boys paddled the boat. Out in the dawn ahead of them the tug puffed a path through the foggy mist. The water was chilly. Mist glistened on top of it. Far out, beyond the buoys, Philip encountered a placid, untroubled sea. The liner, a German tourist boat, was loaded to the bridge. The water was as still as a lake of ice.

"All right, Ernest, let's hurry—"

Philip drew in the oars. The *Kron Prinz Wilhelm* came near. Huddled in thick European coats, the passengers viewed from their lofty estate the spectacle of two naked Negro boys peeping up at them from a wiggly *bateau*.

"Penny, mistah, penny, mistah!"

Somebody dropped a quarter. Ernest, like a shot, flew after it. Half a foot down he caught it as it twisted and turned in the gleaming sea. Vivified by the icy dip, Ernest was a raving wolf and the folk aboard dealt a lavish hand.

"Ovah, yah, mistah," cried Philip, "ovah, yah."

For a Dutch guilder Philip gave an exhibition of "cork." Under something of a ledge on the side of the boat he had stuck a piece of cork. Now, after his and Ernest's mouths were full of coins, he could afford to be extravagant and treat the Europeans to a game of West Indian "cork."

Roughly ramming the cork down in the water, Philip, after the fifteenth ram or so, let it go, and flew back, upwards, having thus "lost" it. It was Ernest's turn now, as a sort of end-man, to scramble forward to the spot where Philip had dug it down and "find" it; the first one to do so, having the prerogative, which he jealously guarded, of raining on the other a series of thundering leg blows. As boys in the West Indies Philip and Ernest had played it. Of a Sunday the Negro fishermen on the Barbadoes coast made a pagan rite of it. Many a Bluetown dandy got his spine cracked in a game of "cork."

With a passive interest the passengers viewed the proceedings. In a game of "cork," the cork after a succession of "rammings" is likely to drift many feet away whence it was first "lost." One had to be an expert, quick, alert, to spy and promptly seize it as it popped up on the rolling waves. Once Ernest got it and endeavored to make much of the possession. But Philip, besides being two feet taller than he, was slippery as an eel, and Ernest, despite all the artful ingenuity at his command, was able to do no more than ineffectively beat the water about him. Again and again he tried, but to no purpose.

Becoming reckless, he let the cork drift too far away from him and Philip seized it.

He twirled it in the air like a crap shooter, and dug deep down in the water with it, "lost" it, then leaped back, briskly waiting for it to rise.

About them the water, due to the ramming and beating, grew restive. Billows sprang up; soaring, swelling waves sent the skiff nearer the shore. Anxiously Philip and Ernest watched for the cork to make its ascent.

It was all a bit vague to the whites on the deck, and an amused chuckle floated down to the boys.

And still the cork failed to come up.

"I'll go after it," said Philip at last, "I'll go and fetch it." And, from the edge of the boat he leaped, his body long and resplendent in the rising tropic sun.

It was a suction sea, and down in it Philip plunged. And it was lazy, too, and willful—the water. Ebony-black, it tugged and mocked. Old brass staves—junk dumped there by the retiring French—thick, yawping mud, barrel hoops, tons of obsolete brass, a wealth of slimy steel faced him. Did a "rammed" cork ever go that deep?

And the water, stirring, rising, drew a haze over Philip's eyes. Had a cuttlefish, an octopus, a nest of eels been routed? It seemed so to Philip, blindly diving, pawing. And the sea, the tide—touching the roots of Deathpool—tugged and tugged. His gathering hands stuck in mud. Iron staves bruised his shins. It was black down there. Impenetrable.

Suddenly, like a flash of lightning, a vision blew across Philip's brow. It was a soaring shark's belly. Drunk on the nectar of the deep, it soared above Philip—rolling, tumbling, rolling. It had followed the boy's scent with the accuracy of a diver's rope.

Scrambling to the surface, Philip struck out for the boat. But the sea, the depths of it wrested out of an aeon's slumber, had sent it a mile from his diving point. And now, as his strength ebbed, a shark was at his heels.

"Shark! Shark!" was the cry that went up from the ship.

Hewing a lane through the hostile sea Philip forgot the cunning of the doddering beast and swam noisier than he needed to. Faster grew his strokes. His line was a straight, dead one. Fancy strokes and dives—giraffe leaps . . . he summoned into play. He shot out recklessly. One time he suddenly paused—and floated for a stretch. Another time he swam on his back, gazing at the chalky sky. He dived for whole lengths.

But the shark, a bloaty, stone-colored mankiller, took a shorter cut. Circumnavigating the swimmer it bore down upon him with the speed of a hurricane. Within adequate reach it turned, showed its gleaming belly, seizing its prey.

A fiendish gargle—the gnashing of bones—as the sea once more closed its jaws on Philip.

Some one aboard ship screamed. Women fainted. There was talk of a gun. Ernest, an oar upraised, capsized the boat as he tried to inflict a blow on the coursing, chop-licking maneater.

And again the fish turned. It scraped the waters with its deadly fins.

At Coco Té, at the fledging of the dawn, Maffi, polishing the tinware, hummed an *obeah* melody

Trinidad is a damn fine place
But *obeah* down dey. . . .

Peace had come to her at last.

The Palm Porch

I

Below, a rock engine was crushing stone, shooting up rivers of steam and signaling the frontier's rebirth. Opposite, there was proof, a noisy, swaggering sort of proof, of the gradual death and destruction of the frontier post. Black men behind wheelbarrows slowly ascended a rising made of spliced boards and emptied the sand rock into the maw of a mixing machine. More black men, a peg down, behind wheelbarrows, formed a line which caught the mortar pouring into the rear organ of the omnivorous monster.

"All, all gone," cried Miss Buckner, and the girls at her side shuddered. All quietly felt the sterile menace of it. There, facing its misery, tears came to Miss Buckner's eyes and a jeweled, half-white hand, lifted gently to give a paltry vision of the immensity of it.

"All of that," she sighed, "all of that was swamp—when I came to the Isthmus. All." A gang of "taw"-pitching boys, sons of the dusky folk seeping up from Caribbean isles, who had first painted Hudson Alley and "G" Street a dense black, and were now spreading up to the Point—swarmed to a spot in the road which the stone crusher had been especially cruel to, and drew a marble ring. Contemptibly pointing to them,

Miss Buckner observed, "a year ago that would have been impossible. I can't understand what the world is coming to." Gazing at one another the girls were not tempted to speak, but were a bit bewildered at this show of grossness on their mother's part. And anyway, it was noon, and they wanted to go to sleep.

But a light, flashed on a virgin past, burst on Miss Buckner, and she became reminiscent. . . .

Dark dense thicket; water paving it. Deer, lions, tigers bounding through it. Centuries, perhaps, of such pure, free rule. Then some khaki-clad, red-faced and scrawny-necked whites deserted the Zone and brought saws to the roots of palmetto, spears to the bush cats and jaguars, lysol to the mosquitoes and flies and tar to the burning timber-swamp. A wild racing to meet the Chagres and explore the high reaches of the Panama jungle. After the torch, ashes and ghosts—bare, black stalks, pegless stumps, flakes of charred leaves and half-burnt tree trunks. Down by a stream watering a village of black French colonials, dredges began to work. More of the Zone pests, rubber-booted ones, tugged out huge iron pipes and safely laid them on the gutty bosom of the swamp. Congeries of them. Then one windy night the dredges began a moaning noise. It was the sea groaning and vomiting. Through the throat of the pipes it rattled, and spat stones—gold and emerald and amethyst. All sorts of juice the sea upheaved. It dug deep down, too, far into the recesses of its sprawling cosmos. Back to a pre-geologic age it delved, and brought up things.

Down by the mouth of a creole stream the dredges worked. Black in the golden mist, black on the lagoon.

With the aftermath there came a dazzling array of corals and jewels—jewels of the griping sea. Magically the sun hardened and whitened it. Sand-white. Brown. Golden. Dross surged up; guava stumps, pine stumps, earth-burned sprats, river stakes. But the crab shell—sea crabs, pink and crimson—the sharks' teeth, blue, and black, and purple ones—the pearls, and glimmering stones—shone brightly.

Upon the lake of jeweled earth dusk swept a mantle of hazy blue.

II

"W'en yo' fadah wake up in de mawnin' time wid' 'im marinah stiff out in front o' him—"

"Mek fun," said Miss Buckner, rising regally, "an' be a dam set o' fools all yo' life." She buried the butt in a Mexican urn, and strode by Anesta sprawling half-robed on the matted floor. "Move, gal, an' le' me go out dey an' show dis black sow how we want 'ar fi' stew de gunga peas an' fowl."

"Oh, me don't wan' fi' go to no pahty," yawned Hyacinth, fingering the pages of a boudoir textbook, left her one evening by an Italian sea captain, "me too tiad, sah."

"An' me can't see how de hell me gwine mek up to any man if me got fi' fling in him face a old blue shif' me did got las' week. W'en is Scipio gwine bring me dat shawl him pramise fi' giv' me?"

"Me no fond ha-tall o' any 'Panish man," cried Anesta, "an' me don't see how me can—"

Miss Buckner swung around, struck. "Yo' t'ink so, he, his dat wha' yo' t'ink? Well, yo' bess mek up unna mind—all o' unna! Well, wha' a bunch o' lazy ongrateful bitches de whole carload of unna is, dough he?"

Suddenly she broke off, anger seaming her brow. "Unna don't know me his hindebted to him, no? Unna don't know dat hif hit wasn't farrim a lot o' t'ings wha' go awn up yah, would be street property long ago—an' some o' we yo' see spo'tin' roun' yah would be some way else, an' diffrant altogaddah."

"Ah know not me."

"Ah know Oi ain't owe nobody nothin'—"

"Yo' think yo' don't! But don't fool yourselves, children, there is more to make the mare go than you think—I see that now."

She busied herself gathering up glasses, flouncing off to the pantry.

The Palm Porch was not a canteen, it was a house. But it was a house of lavish self-containment. It was split up in rooms, following a style of architecture which was the flair of the Isthmian realtors, and each room opened out on the porch. Each had, too, an armor of leafy laces; shining dust and scarlet. Each had its wine and decanters, music and song.

On the squalid world of Colon it was privileged to gaze with hauteur, for Miss Buckner, the owner of the Palm Porch, was a lady of poise, charm and caution. Up around the ribs of the porch she had put a strip of canvas cloth. It shut out eyes effectively. Glancing up, one saw boxes of rosebush and flower vines, but beyond that—nothing. The porch's green paint, the opulent flower pots and growing plants helped to plaster on it the illusion of the tropical jungle.

There clung to Miss Buckner an idea of sober reality. Her hips were full, her hands long, hairy, unfeminine, her breasts dangling. She was fully seven feet tall and had a small, round head. Her hair was close to it—black, curly. Courageously she had bobbed and parted it at a time when it was unseasonable to do so, and yet retain a semblance of respect among the Victorian dames of the Spanish tropics.

Urged on by the ruthless spirit which was a very firm part of her, Miss Buckner was not altogether unaware of the capers she was cutting amid the few beings she actually touched. Among the motley blacks and browns and yellows on the Isthmus, there would be talk—but how was it to drift back to her? Via Zuline? Shame! "Who me? Me talk grossip wit' any sahvant gyrl, if yo' t'ink so yo' lie!" But the lack of an elfin figure and the possession of a frizzly head of hair, was more than made up for by Miss Buckner's gift of *manners*.

"Gahd, wha' she did got it, he?" folk asked; but neither London, nor Paris, nor Vienna answered. Indeed, Miss Buckner, a lady of sixty, would have been *wordless* at the idea of having to go beyond the dickty rim of Jamaica in quest of *manners*. It was absurd to think so. This drop to the Isthmus was Miss Buckner's first gallop across the sea.

And so, like sap to a rubber tree, Miss Buckner's manner clung to her. Upon those of her sex she had slight cause to ply it, for at the Palm Porch few of them were allowed. Traditionally, it was a man's house. When Miss Buckner, beneath a brilliant lorgnette, was gracious enough to look at a man, she looked, sternly, unsmilingly down at him. When of a Sabbath, her hair in oily frills, wearing a silken shawl of cream and red, a dab of vermilion on her mouth, she swept regally down Bolivar Street on the way to the market, maided by the indolent Zuline, she had half of the city gaping at the

animal wonder of her. Brief-worded, cool-headed, by a stab-
bing thrust or a petulant gesture, she'd confound any fish
seller, any dealer in yampi or Lucy yam, cocoanut milk or
red peas—and pass quietly on, untouched by the briny babel.

In fact, from Colon to Cocoa Grove the pale-faced folk
who drank sumptuously in the bowl of life churned by her
considered Miss Buckner a woman to tip one's hat to—regal
rite—a woman of taste and culture. Machinists at Balboa,
engineers at Miraflores, sun-burned sea folk gladly testified
to that fact. All had words of beauty for the ardor of Miss
Buckner's salon.

Of course one gathered from the words which came like
blazing meteors out of her mouth that Miss Buckner would
have liked to be white; but, alas! she was only a mulatto. No
one had ever heard of her before she and her five daughters
moved into the Palm Porch. It was to be expected, the world
being what it is, that words of murmured treason would
drift abroad. A wine merchant, Raymond de la Croix, and a
Jamaica horse breeder, Walter de Paz, vowed they had seen
her at an old seaman's bar on Matches Lane serving ale and
ofttimes more poetic things than ale to young blond-headed
Britons who would especially go there. But de Paz and de la
Croix were men of frustrated idealism, and their words, to
Miss Buckner at least, brutal though they were, were swept
aside as expressions of useless chatter. Whether she was the
result of a union of white and black, French and Spanish,
English and Maroon—no one knew. Of an equally mystical
heritage were her daughters, creatures of a rich and shining beauty. Of their father the less said the better. And in
the absence of data tongues began to wag. Norwegian bos'n.

Jamaica lover—Island triumph. Crazy Kingston nights. To the lovely young ladies in question it was a subject to be religiously highhatted and tabooed. The prudent Miss Buckner, who had a burning contempt for statistics, was a trifle hazy about the whole thing.

One of the girls, white as a white woman, eyes blue as a Viking maid's, had eloped, at sixteen, to Miss Buckner's eternal disgust, with a shiny-armed black who had at one time been sent to the Island jail for the proletarian crime of praedial larceny. The neighbors swore it had been love at first sight. But it irked and maddened Miss Buckner. "It a dam pity shame," she had cried, dabbing a cologned handkerchief to her nose, "it a dam pity shame."

Another girl, the eldest of the lot (Miss Buckner had had seven in all), had, O! ages before, given birth to a pretty, gray-eyed baby boy, when she was but seventeen and—again to Miss Buckner's disgust—had later taken up with a willing young mulatto, a Christian in the Moravian Church. He was an able young man, strong and honest, and wore shoes, but Miss Buckner almost went mad—groaned at the pain her daughters caused her. "Oh, me Gahd," she had wept, "Oh, me Gahd, dem ah send me to de dawgs—dem ah send me to de dawgs." He was but a clerk in the cold storage; sixty dollars a month—wages of an accursed silver employee. Silver is nigger; nigger is silver. Nigger-silver. Why, roared Miss Buckner, stockings could not be bought with that, much more take care of a woman accustomed to "foxy clothes an' such" and a dazzling baby boy. Silver employee! Bah! Why couldn't he be a "Gold" one? Gold is white; white is gold. Gold-white! "Gold," and get $125 a month, like "de fella nex' tarrim, he?

Why, him had to be black, an' get little pay, an' tek way me gal picknee from me? Now, hanswah me dat!" Nor did he get coal and fuel free, besides. He had to dig down and pay extra for them. He was not, alas! white. Which hurt, left Miss Buckner cold; caused her nights of sleepless despair. Wretch! "To t'ink a handsam gal like dat would-ah tek up wi' a dam black neygah man like him, he, w'en she could a stay wit' me 'n do bettah." But few knew the secret of Miss Buckner's sorrow, few sensed the deep tragedy of her.

And so, to dam the flood of tears, Miss Buckner and the remaining ones of her flamingo brood, had drawn up at the Palm Porch. All day, the sun burning a flame through the torrid heavens, they would be postured on the porch. Virgin to the sun's gentle caresses, with the plants and flowers keeping the heat at bay, they'd be there. Slippers dangled on the tips of restive toes. Purple-lined kimonos falling away gave access to blushing, dimpled bodies. Great fine tresses of hair, the color of night, gave shadows to the revelations, gave structure.

III

"Come, Zuline,—hurry—it's getting late." The porch was vacant, dusk had fallen, and Miss Buckner wore an evening gown of white taffeta, fashioned in the Victorian epoch. It was tight and stiff and created a rustle, and there was a black bandeau pasted on to her skull.

Sullenly the girl came, and gathered up the debris. "Sweep up dis ash, an cayh dis slip in Goldy's room, de careless t'ing," said Miss Buckner.

She went to one of the dusk-flooded rooms and seized

a studded dagger which she stuck among the watches and brooches which shone on her bosom. She patted it, made sure it was safely a part of the glittering pattern and ordered the night on.

"Get up, girls," she shouted, invading room after room, "it is late, get up!"

"Hello, Sailor Mack. Hit any home runs to-day?"

"An' you, you Kentucky millionaire—how many ships came through the locks to-day?"

"Bullocks—did you say?"

"Fie!"

"Oh, Mistah Council," she said, "how do you do?" Young Briton, red-faced, red-eyed, red-haired. Yellow-teethed, dribble-lipped, swobble-mouthed, bat-eared.

He kissed the proffered hand, and bowed low. He was gallant, and half-drunk. "Where's my girl, Anesta," he said, "by God, she is the sweetest woman, black or white—on the whole goddamed—"

"Sh, be quiet, son, come," and Miss Buckner led him to a chair among a group of men.

Constantly, Miss Buckner's hand kept fluttering to the diamond-headed pin stuck in her bosom.

Chaos prevailed, but Miss Buckner was quite sober. All about there were broken vases, overturned flower-pots, flowers, women's shoes. All the men were prostrate, the women exultant.

As midnight approached, the doorbell suddenly rang. And Miss Buckner rose, cautioning serenity. "All right, boys, let's have less noise—the captain's comin'."

In Anesta's lap there was an eruption, a young Vice-

Consul staggered up—shaking her off, ready to face the coming of the visitor.

"Sit down, Baldy," she implored, "come back here to me—"

"Skipper, eh? Who is he? Wha' ya hell tub is he on?" He was tall and his body rocked menacingly.

"Put that goddam lime juicer to bed, somebody, will ya?"

"Yo' gawd dam American—why—"

Anesta rose, flying to him. "Now, Tommy," she said, patting his cheek, "that isn't nice."

"Let the bleddy bastard go to—"

But apparently an omnipotent being had invaded the porch, and a deep-throated voice barked sweetly down it, "Anesta, darling, take Baldy inside, and come here!"

"But, mother—"

"Do as you are told, darling, and don't waste any more time."

"No, Gawd blarst yo'—nobody will slip off these pants of mine. Lemme go!"

"Be a gentleman, sweet, and behave."

"What a hell of a ruction it are, eh?"

"Help me wit' 'im, Hyacinth—"

Ungallantly yielding, he permitted the girl to force him along on her arm. He stepped in the crown of Mr. Thingamerry's hat. Only yesterday he had put on a gleaming white suit. Done by the Occupation, the starch on the edges of it made it dagger sharp. Now it was a sight; ugly drink stains darkened it. Booze, perspiration, tobacco weeds moistened it. His shirt, once stiff, was black and wrinkled. His tie, his collar and trousers awry. His fire-red hair was wet and bushy and rumpled. Black curses fell from his mouth. But six months in the tropics and the nights and the girls at the Palm Porch had overpowered him. Held him tight. Sent from Liverpool to the British Consulate at Colon, he had fallen for the languor of the seacoast, he had been seized by the magic glow of the Palm Porch.

Seeing the Captain, Miss Buckner was as bright-eyed as a débutante. Instinctively her hands fled to her beaming bosom, but now the impulse was guided by a soberer circumstance.

The Captain was smiling. "Well, good lady," he said, "I see you are as charming and as nervous as usual. I hope you have good news for me to-day." He bowed very low, and kissed the jeweled hand.

"Oh, dear Captain," exclaimed Miss Buckner, touched by the Spaniard's gentility, "of course I have!" And she went on, "My renowned friend, it is so splendid of you to come. We have been looking forward to seeing you every minute—really. Was I not, Anesta, dear?" She turned, but the girl was nowhere in sight. "Anesta? Anesta, my dear? Where are you?"

It was a risky job, wading through the lanes of wine-fat men. As she and the Captain sped along, she was careful to let him see that she admired his golden epaulets, and the lofty contemptible way he'd step over the drunken Britons, but she in her own unobtrusive way was hurling to one side every one that came in contact with her.

"Christ was your color. Christ was olive—Jesus Christ was a man of olive—"

"Won't you wait a moment, Captain—I'll go and get Anesta." And she left him.

About him tossed the lime-juicers, the "crackers"—wine-crazed, woman-crazed. He turned in disgust, and drew out an open-worked handkerchief, blowing his nose contemptuously. He was a handsome man. He was dusky, sun-browned, vain. He gloried in a razor slash he had caught on his right cheek in a brawl over a German slut in a District canteen. It served to intensify the glow women fancied in him. When he laughed it would turn pale, stark pale, when he was angry, it oozed red, blood-red.

Miss Buckner returned like a whirlwind, blowing and applying a Japanese fan to her bosom.

In replacing it, a crimson drop had fallen among the gathering of emeralds and pearls, but it was nothing for her to be self-conscious about.

Very gladly she drew close to him, smiling. "Now, you hot-blooded Latin," she said, the pearls on the upper row of her teeth shining brighter than ever, "you must never give up the chase! The Bible says 'Him that is exalted' . . . the gods will never be kind to you if you don't have patience. . . . No use . . . you won't understand . . . the Bible. Come!"

Pointing to the human wreckage through which they had swept, she turned, "In dear old Kingston, Captain, none of this sort of thing ever occurred! None! And you can imagine how profusely it constrains me!"

"Anesta, where are you, my dear? Here's the Captain —waiting."

Out of a room bursting with the pallor of night the girl came. Her grace and beauty, the tumult of color reddening her, excited the Captain. Curtseying, she paused at the door, one hand at her throat, the other held out to him.

It was butter in the Captain's mouth, and Miss Buckner, at the door, viewing the end of a very strategic quest, felt happy. The Captain, after all, was such a naughty boy!

The following day the *policia* came and got Tommy's body. Over the blood-black hump a sheet was flung. It dabbed up the claret. The natives tilted their chins unconcernedly at it.

Firm in the Captain's graces Miss Buckner was too busy to be excited by the spectacle. In fact, Miss Buckner, while Zuline sewed a button on her suède shoes, was endeavoring to determine whether she'd have chocolate soufflé or maidenhair custard for luncheon that afternoon.

Subjection

Of a sudden the sun gave Ballet an excuse to unbend and straighten himself up, his young, perspiring back cricking in the upward swing. He hurled the pick furiously across the dusty steel rail, tugged a frowsy, sweat-moist rag out of his overall pocket and pushed back his cap, revealing a low, black brow embroidered by scraps of crisp, straggly hair. He fastened, somewhat obliquely, white sullen eyes on the Marine. Irrefutably, by its ugly lift, Ballet's mouth was in on the rising rebellion which thrust a flame of smoke into the young Negro's eyes.

"Look at he, dough," he said, "takin' exvantage o' de po' lil' boy. A big able hog like dat."

Toro Point resounded to the noisy rhythm of picks swung by gnarled black hands. Sunbaked rock stones flew to dust, to powder. In flashing unison rippling muscle glittered to the task of planing a mound of rocky earth dredged up on the barren seashore.

Songs seasoned the rhythm. And the men sang on and swung picks, black taciturn French colonials, and ignored Ballet, loafing, beefing. . . .

The blows rained. The men sang—blacks, Island blacks—Turks Island, St. Vincent, the Bahamas—

Diamond gal cook fowl botty giv' de man

"I'll show you goddam niggers how to talk back to a white man—"

About twelve, thirteen, fourteen men, but only the wind rustled. A hastening breath of wind, struck dead on the way by the grueling presence of the sun.

A ram-shackle body, dark in the ungentle spots exposing it, jogged, reeled and fell at the tip of a white bludgeon. Forced a dent in the crisp caked earth. An isolated ear lay limp and juicy, like some exhausted leaf or flower, half joined to the tree whence it sprang. Only the sticky milk flooding it was crimson, crimsoning the dust and earth.

"Unna is a pack o' men, ni'," cried Ballet, outraged, "unna see de po' boy get knock' down an' not a blind one o' wunna would a len' he a han'. Unna is de mos'—"

But one man, a Bajan creole, did whip up the courage of voice. "Good God, giv' he a chance, ni'. Don' kick he in de head now he is 'pon de groun'—" and he quickly, at a nudge and a hushed, "Hey, wha' do you? Why yo' don't tek yo' hand out o' yo' matey' saucepan?" from the only other creole, lapsed into ruthless impassivity.

"Hey, you!" shouted Ballet at last loud enough for the Marine to hear, "why—wha' you doin'? Yo' don' know yo' killin' dat boy, ni'?"

"Le' all we giv' he a han' boys—"

"Ah know I ain't gwine tetch he."

"Nor me."

"Nor me needah."

"Who gwine giv' me a han', ni'?"

"Ain't gwine get myself in no trouble. Go mixin' meself in de backra dem business—"

"Hey, Ballet, if yo' know wha' is good fo' yo'self, yo' bess min' yo' own business, yo' hear wha' me tell yo', yah."

"Wha' yo' got fi' do wit' it? De boy ain't got no business talkin' back to de marinah man—"

"Now he mek up he bed, let 'im lie down in it."

Shocked at sight of the mud the marine's boots left on the boy's dusty, crinkly head, Ballet mustered the courage of action. Some of the older heads passed on, awed, incredulous.

"Yo' gwine kill dat boy," said Ballet, staggering up to the marine.

"You mind yer own goddam business, Smarty, and go back to work," said the marine. He guided an unshaking yellow-spotted finger under the black's warm, dilating nostrils. "Or else—"

He grew suddenly deathly pale. It was a pallor which comes to men on the verge of murder. Mouth, the boy at issue, one of those docile, half-white San Andres coons, was a facile affair. Singly, red-bloodedly one handled it. But here, with this ugly, thick-lipped, broad-chested upstart, there was need for handling of an errorless sort.

"I'll git you yet," the marine said, gazing at Ballet quietly, "I'll fill you full of lead yet, you black bastard!"

"Why yo' don't do it now," stuttered Ballet, taking a hesitating step forward, "yo' coward, yo'—a big able man lik' yo' beatin' a lil' boy lik' dat. Why yo' don' hit me? Betcha yo' don' put down yo' gun an' fight me lik' yo' got any guts."

The marine continued to stare at him. "I'll git you yet,"

he said, "I'll git you yet, Smarty, don't kid yourself." And he slowly moved on.

The boy got up. The sun kept up its irrepressible sizzling. The men minded their business.

Ballet, sulking, aware of the marine on the stony hedge, aware of the red, menacing eyes glued on him, on every single move he made, furtively broke rocks.

"Boy, yo' ain't gwine t' wuk teeday, ni'? Git up!"

Exhausted by the orgy of work and evensong, Ballet snored, rolled, half asleep.

"Get up, ni' yo' ain't hear de *korchee* blowin' fi' go to wuk, ni?"

"Ugh—ooo—ooo"

"Yo' ent hear me, ni? Um is six o'clock, boy, get up befo' yo' is late. Yo' too lazy, get up, a big, lazy boy lik' yo'—"

Sitting at the head of the cot, a Bible in one hand, Ballet's mother kept shaking him into wakefulness. In the soft flush of dawn bursting in on the veranda, Mirrie's restless gummoist eyes fell on her son's shining black shoulders. He was sprawled on the canvas, a symbol of primordial force, groaning, half-awake.

"Hey, wha' is to become o' dis boy, ni?" she kept on talking to the emerging flow of light, "Why yo' don't go to bed at night, ni? Stayin' out evah night in de week. Spanishtown, Spanishtown, Spanishtown, evah night—tek heed, ni, tek heed, yo' heah—when yo' run into trouble don' come an' say Ah didn't tell yo'."

To Ballet this was the song of eternity. From the day Mirrie discovered through some vilely unfaithful source the moments there were for youths such as he, in the crimson shades of *el barrio*, the psalms of rage and despair were chanted to him.

His thin, meal-yellow singlet stiffened, ready to crack. He continued snoring. Frowsy body *fuses*, night sod, throttled the air on the dingy narrow porch on which they both contrived to sleep.

She shook him again. 'Get up—yo' hear de *korchee* blowin' fo' half pas' six. Time to go to wuk, boy."

Ballet slowly rose—the lower portions of him arching upwards.

The dome of the equator swirled high above Colon—warmth, sticky sweat, heat, malaria, flies—here one slept coverless. Mechanically uttering words of prayer drilled into him by Mirrie, he raised himself up on the stain-blotched cot, salaamed, while Mirrie piously turned her face to the sun.

When he had finished, Ballet, still half asleep, angled his way into his shirt, dragged on his blue pants, took down the skillet from the ledge and went to the cess-pool to bathe his face.

"Yo' know, mahmie," he said to Mirrie as he returned, wiping his eyes with the edge of his shirt sleeve, "I don't feel lik' goin' to work dis mornin'—"

"Why, bo?"

"Oh, Ah dunno." He sat down to tea.

"Yo' too lazy," she blurted out. "Yo' want to follow all o' dem nasty vagabonds an' go roun' de streets an' interfere wit' people. Yo' go to work, sah, an' besides, who is to feed me if yo' don't wuk? Who—answer me dat! Boy, yo' bes' mek up yo' min' an' get under de heel o' de backra."

Peeling the *conkee* off the banana leaf encasing it, Ballet's glistening half-dried eyes roved painfully at the austere lines on his mother's aged face.

"Ah don' wan' fo' go—"

"Dah is wha' Ah get fo' bringin' unna up. Ungrateful vagybond! Dah is wha' Ah get fo' tyin' up my guts wit' plantation trash, feedin' unna—jes' lik' unna wuthliss pappy. But yo' go long an' bring me de coppers when pay day come. Dah is all Ah is axin' yo' fo' do. Ah too old fo' wash de backra dem dutty ole clothes else unna wouldn't hav' to tu'n up unna backside when Ah ax unna fo' provide anyt'ing fo' mah."

"Oh, yo' mek such a fuss ovah nutton," he sulked.

A stab of pain corrugated Ballet's smooth black brow. His mother's constant dwelling on the dearth of the family fortunes produced in him a sundry set of emotions—escape in rebellion and refusal to do as against a frenzied impulse to die retrieving things.

The impulse to do conquered, and Ballet rose, seized the skillet containing the *conkee* for his midday meal and started.

A fugitive tear, like a pendant pearl, paused on Mirrie's wrinkled, musk-brown face.

"Son, go' long—an tek care o' yo'self."

Light-heartedly Ballet galloped down the stairs. Halfway to the garbage-strewn piazza, he paused to lean over the banister and peep into the foggy depths of the kitchen serving the occupants of the bawdy rooms on the street-level of the tenement.

"Up orready?" shouted Ballet, throwing a sprig of cane peeling at a plump black figure engaged in the languid task of turning with a long flat piece of board a *tache* of bubbling starch.

In a disorderly flight to the piazza one foot landed on the seed of a part-skinned alligator pear. He deftly escaped a fall. Quickly righting himself, he made for the misty, stewy inclosure—dashing under clothes lines, overturning a bucket of wash blue, nearly bursting a hole in some one's sunning, gleaming sheet.

Dark kitchen; slippery and smoky; unseen vermin and strange upgrowth of green snaky roots swarmed along the sides of washtubs, turpentine cans, *taches*, stable ironware.

Presiding over one of the *taches* was a girl. She was slim, young, fifteen years old. Her feet were bare, scales, dirt black, dirt white, sped high up her legs. The fragment of a frock, some peasant thing, once colored, once flowered, stood stiff, rigid off the tips of her curving buttocks.

Grazing the ribs of the *tache* with the rod, Blanche, blithely humming

> Wha' de use yo' *gwine* shawl up
> Now dat yo' character gone—
> Dicky jump, Dicky jump
> Ah wan' fi' lie down!

was unaware of Ballet slowly crouching behind her.

Becoming clairvoyantly tongue-tied, Blanche suddenly turned, and Ballet came up to her.

Exerting a strange ripe magic over him, the girl cried, "Yo' frighten me, Ballet, how yo' dey?

"Too bad 'bout las' night," she said, in the low lulling tones of a West Indian servant girl, lifting not an eyebrow, and continuing to stir the thickening starch.

"An' me had me min' 'pon it so bad," the boy said, an intense gleam entering his eyes.

"So it dey," responded Blanche, "sometime it hav' obtusions, de neddah time de road are clear."

"Dat a fac'," the boy concurred sorrowfully, "it fatify de *coza* so dat a man can ha'dly sit down an' say 'well, me gwine do dis dis minute an' me gwine do dis dat,' fo' de devil is jes' as smaht as de uddah man uptop."

"Up cose," said Blanche in her most refined manner, "Ah, fi' me notion is to tek de milk fom de cow when him are willin' fi' giv' it, wheddah it are in de mawnin' time or in de even' time—"

"Wha' yo' are doin', Ballet, wait—let me put down de stick—wait, Ah say—yo' in a hurry?"

"Wha' Sweetbread, dey? Him gone t' wuk orready?"

"Yes—me don' know but it are seem to me lik' some time muss eclapse befo' dere is any life ah stir in dis kitchen—"

"Oh, Blanche!"

"Yo' bes' be careful, Ballet, fo' de las' time Ah had fi' scrouch aroun' fi' hooks an' eyes an' dat dyam John Chinaman 'im not gwine giv' me any-t'ing beout me giv' 'im somet'ing."

"All right—dere—Blanche—wait—"

"Yo' know what 'im say to me de uddah dey? Me wuz—wait, tek yo' time, Ballet, de cock is jus' a crow, it are soon yet—oh, don't sweet—

"'Im say to me dat Ah mus' giv' 'im somet'ing. An' me say to 'im, 'but John, yo' no me husban'—'an' yo' know wha' de dyam yallah rascal say 'im say 'but me no fo' yo' husban' too'?"

Her hair was hard, but the marble floor of the kitchen undoubtedly helped to stiffen its matty, tangled plaits. And in spite of the water daily splashing over the tanks and *taches* on to the ground, her strong young body took nothing diminishing from it. Only, unquestioningly the force of such a wiry, gluey, gummy impact as theirs left her heels a little broader, and a readier prey for chiggers, by virtue of the constantly widening crevices in them, her hair a little more difficult to comb and her dress in a suspiciously untidy mood.

Emerging from the slippery darkness of the kitchen, Ballet dashed up Eighth Street. A Colon sunrise streamed in on its lazy inert life. Opposite, some of the disciples of the High Priest of the Ever-Live, Never-Die Sect sat moping, not fully recovered from the flowing mephitic languor of the evening's lyrical excesses.

All the way up the street, Ballet met men of one sort or another trekking to work—on tipsy depot wagons, shovels, picks, forks sticking out like spikes; on foot, alone, smoking pipes, hazily concerned.

Grog shops, chink stores and brothels were closed. The tall, bare, paneled doors were fastened. The sun threw warmth and sting under verandas; shriveled banana peels to crusts; darkened the half-eaten chunks of soft pomegranates left by some extravagant epicurean, gave manna to big husky wasps foregathering wherever there was light, sun, warmth. . . .

Up on the verandas there dark, bright-skirted, flame-lipped girls, the evening before, danced in squares, holding up the tips of their flimsy dresses, to the *coombia* of creole island places. Creole girls led, thwarted, wooed and burned by *obeah*-working, weed-smoking St. Lucian men. Jamaica girls, fired by an inextinguishable warmth, danced, whirling, wheeling, rolling, rubbing, spinning their posteriors and their hips, in circles, their breasts like rosettes of flame, quivering to the rhythm of the *mento*—conceding none but the scandalously sexless. Spanish girls, white ones, yellow ones, brown ones, furiously gay, furiously concerned over the actualities of beauty.

Over a bar of dredged in earth, Ballet sped. In the growing sunlight figures slowly made for the converging seacoast.

Work-folk yelled to Ballet tidings of the dawn. . . .

"Why yo' don' tek de chiggahs out o' yo' heel an' walk lik' yo' got life in yo' body—"

"Yo' gwine be late, too."

"Yo' go 'long, bo, Oi ent hurrin' fo' de Lawd Gawd Heself dis mawnin'—"

Ahead a vision of buxom green cocoa palms spread like a crescent—from the old rickety wooden houses walled behind the preserves of the quarantine station all the way past the cabins of the fishing folk and dinky bathhouses for the blacks to the unseemly array of garbage at the dump. Out to the seacoast and the writhing palms swarmed men from Coolie Town, Bottle Alley, Bolivar Street, Boca Grande, Silver City.

As he approached the edge of the sea, Ballet waded through grass which rose higher and thicker, whose dew lay in glimmering crystal moistures. Beyond the palm trees opened a vista of the river, the color of brackish water. Empty cocoanut husks cluttered the ground. Sitting on upturned canoes men smoked pipes and sharpened tools, murmuring softly. All across the bay labor boats formed a lane, a lane to Toro Point, shining on the blue horizon.

Drawing nearer the crux of things, Mouth ran up to Ballet and put an unsteady, excited grip on his shoulder.

"Ballet, bettah don' go t' wuk teeday—"

Scorn and disdain crossed Ballet's somber black face.

"Wha' is dah?" he said, refusing to hear his ears.

"Ah, say, don' go t' wuk teeday—stan' home—"

"Why, boy?"

"Dah marine is lookin' fo' yo'."

"Lookin' fo' me?" Ballet stuck a skeptical finger in the pit of his stomach. "Wha' he lookin' fo' me fo'?" A quizzical frown creased his brow.

"He say yo' had no business to jook yo' mout' in de ruction yestiddy. Dat yo' too gypsy an' if yo' know bes' fo' yo'self—"

"Oh, le' he come," cried Ballet, "de blind coward, le' he come—"

A ruffian Q. M., paced up and down the water front, brandishing a staff, firing skyrockets of tobacco spit to right and left, strode up. "Don't stand there, boys, getta move on! Jump in this boat—another one's coming—no time to waste—jump in there!"

A marine lieutenant, pistol in hand, superintended the embarkment. A squad of khakied men paraded the strip of seashore.

Ballet joined the cowed obedient retinue limping to the boats. Curiously, in the scramble to embark the water boy got lost.

"Oh, Oi ain't do nutton. Can't do me nutton."

The passage was swift and safe through swelling seas growing darker and deadlier as the tide mounted. Glumly the men sat, uttering few words, standing up as the boat neared the other side of the river and jumping prematurely ashore, getting their feet wet.

Men gathered on pump cars and on the Toro Point river

edge sawing wood to help clear the jungle or sharpening their machetes.

Gangs were forming. Driven by marines, platoons of black men went to obscure parts of the Toro Point bush to cut paths along the swirling lagoon back to the Painted City. Fierce against the sun moaning men jogged with drills on their backs, pounding to dust tons of mortared stone paving lanes through the heathen unexplored jungle.

In the crowd of men, Ballet saw a face leering at him. It was a white face—the face of a scowling marine. . . .

Rockingly, dizzily, it glowed up at him. He was freckled, the pistol in his belt carelessly at hand and he slovenly sported a bayonet rifle.

"Hey—you—I'm talking to you—"

Afraid, unable to fathom the gleam penetrating the depths of the man's eyes, Ballet started running.

"Stand up and take yer medicine, yer goddam skunk," cried the marine; "hey, stop that man—"

Nothing for a black boy, probably a laborer, or a water boy, to do a hide and seek with a tipsy marine. . . .

"Stop that man—"

Ballet flew. He scaled hurdles. He bumped into men. Ugly French colonial words, epithets deserving of a dog, were hurled at him. Impatient, contemptuous Jamaican, colored by a highly British accent, caught at him like shreds.

About to penetrate the dense interior of the jungle, the men sang, soothed the blades of their cutlasses, sang pioneer sea songs, pioneer gold songs. . . .

Comin' Ah tell yo'!
One mo' mawin', buoy,

There was a toolshed set a little ways in. Into it Ballet burst. But a hut, it yet had an "upstairs," and up these the boy scrambled wildly.

Behind a wagon wheel sent up there to the wheelwright to be mended, Ballet, breathing hard, heard the marine enter.

Downstairs. A pause. A search. The top of a barrel blammed shut. Imagine—a boy in a barrel of tar. Ludicrous—laughter snuffed out. Heavy steps started upward, upward. . . .

"Where the hell are yer, yer lousy bastard—yer—come sticking in yer mouth where yer hadn't any goddam business? Minding somebody else's business. I'll teach you niggers down here how to talk back to a white man. Come out o' there, you black bastard."

Behind the wheel, bars dividing the two, Ballet saw the dread khaki—the dirt-caked leggings.

His vision abruptly darkened.

Vap, vap, vap—

Three sure, dead shots.

In the Canal Record, the Q. M. at Toro Point took occasion to extol the virtues of the Department which kept the number of casualties in the recent native labor uprising down to one.

The Black Pin

I

"Wha' dah Alfie got in 'e han'?"

"It ent nutton," spoke up Din, "yo' is ah 'larmer, dah is wha' yo' is."

"Orright den," replied Mirrie, "Oi muss be blin'."

"Like dah is anything de worl' don' know orready."

"Wha' yo' got dey, boy?" murmured April, bent over the washtub, soap suds frosting on her veiny brown arms. She caught up the bulk of her starch-crusted patchwork frock and dried her hands in it.

"Oi tell yo' de boy got somet'ing," Mirrie said, "yo' is such a ownway somebody yo' can't even hear yo' ears ringin'."

"Hey, it muss be a cockroach."

"Or a forty-leg—"

"It ent!"

"Look out deah, boy, yo' gwine stump yo' toe. Bam—tell yo' so! Go help 'e up, Mirrie."

". . . won't stay whe' yo' belong, ni? Why yo' got to be runnin' 'bout de gap like yo' ent got nobody? Like yo' is some sheep who ent got no muddah or no faddah. Come yah, wha' yo' got in yo' han'? Lemmah see it!"

"Woy, woy, it nearly jook mah fingah!"

"Um is a black pin!" exlaimed Mirrie in terror.

"Wha' yo' get dis pin from, boy?" asked April, paling and pausing, then venomously seizing it.

"*Obeah!*"

"Heaven help mah!"

"Who giv' yo' dis pin, boy?" April insisted. Her brows were wrinkled; she exposed the pin to the sun.

"Open yo' mout', boy," she said, "whe' yo' get dis pin?"

"Miss Diggs giv' it to me, mum," murmured Alfie slowly, afraidly.

"Zink Diggs?"

"Yassum."

"Whelp!"

"Giv' yo' dis pin? Wha' fo'? Wha' she giv' yo' a pin fo'? Hey, boy, tek um back to she."

"Sen' he back wit' um!"

"Wha' she mean, yes?"

"Yo' too stupid," shouted Mirrie, assuming an air of worldly wisdom not wholly unsuited to her. "She is wukkin' obeah fo' yo', dat is wha' is de mattah."

"De bad-minded wretch!" cried April. "Hey, wha' Ah do she, ni? Did Ah tek wey she man? Did Ah break she sugar stick? Did Ah call she teef? Did Ah steal she guamazelli plum f'om she? Hey, Ah can't understan' it, yes. Wha' she wan' fo' giv' me a black pin, fo'?"

April held the ghastly symbol against the ripe Barbados sun. Moving in the shadow of the spreading *dounz* she stared at it long and hard. Dark April, a lanky, slipshod woman in a half-dry print skirt and old, sprawling, ratty shoes, stood up, amazed at the lurid import. "Ah wondah why she sen' me dis," she pondered, bewildered.

At her side one of the girls shuffled, cracking the dark, crisp dirt under her feet. "Yo' too stupid," she said. "Little as I is I know wha' um mean."

In something of a trance April went to the shed roof. Cooing pigeons and doves swarmed upon it. Beaten by the rain, dung spattered upon it, ran white and dark blue. Under the shingled edges of the roof bats took refuge. White-spotted canaries sang to the lovely robins poised on the bowing limbs of the *dounz*.

". . . let she alone, sha', g'way."

"Eatin' de po' dog bittle."

"It ent."

"It is."

"Yo' chirrun, behav' unna-self!" April turned, an angry look flooding her dusky face. "Oi gwine beat all yo', yes."

Devil-symbol, *obeah*-symbol—a black pin. "Gwine stick um yah." She bored it into a sunless, rainless spot in the side of the shed roof. "All yo' ent gwine tetch dis pin, unna understan'? Unna heah wha' Oi say? Nobody ent gwine tetch dis pin! If anybody tetch it, they bess get ready fo' tetch me. Oi tell unna dah f'um now."

"Oi know Oi ent gwine got nutton fo' do wit' it."

"Nor me."

"Nor me needah."

"Da, da, unna bess not, fo' Oi'll wash unna behind de fuss one wha' do."

II

Blue cassava—unfit for cakes—about to be grated and pressed for its starch; withering twigs, half-ripe turnips, *bolonjays* a languid flush of green and purple, a graveler—a watery, cork-light potato endwardly dangling; a greedy sow, tugging at a stake, a crusty, squib-smoked "touch bam"— hand-magic, earth-magic, magic of the sun, magic of the moon, magic of the flowing Barbadian gap.

Soft, round, ash-gray, dark violet, purple peas—peas Alfie and Ona and Din and Mirrie ate raw; grown by her own nimble, prolific hands.

Only—the soft quiet of Goddard's Village. Demerara (Mud-Head Land) to Barbadoes . . . on a barque, owned by a West Indian "speckahlatah"—dealer in sweet and Irish spuds—aboard ship, ashore, January to December, wearing thick British tweed, baggy, hairy, scratchy and hot. On the zigaboo's boat April had taken flight. Soft nights; nights of ebony richness; of godless splendor. On the shining waters— blue, frosty, restful—a vision of Jesus walked.

An' crown-un-un Him Lahd av ahl
An' crown-un-un Him Lahd av ahl
An' crown-un-un Him Lahd av ahl
An' Crown Him!
Crown Him!
Lahd!
Av!
Ahl!

The bow of the ship jammed against a brilliant Barbadian sunset, April, a pique shawl swathing her aching body, saw a wiggling *queriman* resist being dragged up on the smooth, spotless deck. Kingfish, sprat, flying fish— sprang, fought, grew enraged at the proximity of sea-less earth. On a half-dry mattress the children slept . . . sucked on sour plums. . . . One more sunset, and the noisy, dusty music of Bridgetown.

All for the remote joys of a gap in Goddard's Village, and of a rosier one: sending the children to school and to St. Stephen's Chapel.

Accomplishing it had been a tear-drenching ordeal.

Up above the brace of stone, up above Waterford's, beyond The Turning, up a dazzling white dusty road, sugar canes on either side of it, an old ox-cart driver at Locust Hall had had an empty shack crumbling slowly on the side of the slanting grass hill. Under the rigid hammering of the sun, with a strip of swamp land below—shy of lady canes, with a rich ornate green—the green of fat juicy canes—the shack was slowly perishing. On hot days centipedes, and scorpions, and white mice, and mongooses prowled possessively through it. On wet ones raining winds dumped on the roof flowers, tree-drips, soggy leaves.

Thirteen sovereigns the man had asked, and she had given him seven. Parts of the house, visibly the beams and foundations, of oak, fell to dust at the touch of the husky black movers, men used to the muscle-straining task of loading ox carts with hefts of loose sugar cane. Husky black movers moaning:

Jam Belly, Quakah Belly,
Swell like a cocoa,
Tee hey, tee hey—
Sally brings grass in yah!

Untouched by the noise, and the heat, and swarming of cane dust, a centipede ran up one of the men's legs. Bawling. Scratching. Portions of the gabling roof lifted on to the dray sagged and dragged all the way to Goddard's Village. From Locust Hall it scraped the ground. Behind it, April, and Alfie and Mirrie and Ona and Din—sagged through the heavy oceans of stone dust.

Of the star apples and *dounz* sunset carved a framework of purple mist. Etched, flung upon the sky. On a stone step Bay Rum, a worker in marl, twanged a guitar; beyond the dingy cabin the ragged edges of an old mortar house were imprisoned against the glowing sky. In the imminent dusk cane arrows swung to and fro, on some peasant farmer's hedge. A donkey cart, wagged in and wagged on, down to the eternity of the gap.

April explored the waterholes along the gap for stones to prop her house on. Some had to be cut, shaved, made small. Hoisting it, smoothing the floor—was a man's job. Plenty of stones, dug up, stolen, at night or early dawn, from obscure vacant spots in the village, to be used in myriad ways. That done, the hammering began. At Locust Hall it must have been a magnet for rusty nails. It took more muscle than was at the command of a woman to swing them out of their sockets. Often an adamant one sent April reeling against the breadfruit tree. Did she have to take them out, at all? Yes. No old nails in her house for her. Wall pockets, too, had to be put in. The lamp, a brilliant one, was crowned with a violet dome.

III

Down through the spine of the lane was a watercourse. Fish—blue, gold, crimson—whirled languidly in it. And from the watercourse sounds came. Busy buttering the soft part that was not exposed to the sun, of the banana leaf into which she was to spread the cornmeal and spice and molasses and then tightly fold to make the *conkee*, April was quick to hear it. The kids squabbling again.

She put down the platter and made for the watercourse. Zenona, the nanny goat, scampered away at her rustling approach.

"Alfie, wha' is it?" she cried, running up.

"He hit my Crump," said Zink Diggs, bivouacked on the fringe of the land, a switch twirling in her hand.

"It ent!" the boy retorted, crying.

"Who tell he fo' hit my Crump?"

"He han' too fast."

"Are dat so?" said April, boiling with rage. "Hey, a big neygah uman like yo' hit a little boy like dis. Yo' ort to be ashamed o' yo' dutty self." She clasped the boy against her knees. He was slyly eying, through a shiny mist, Crump's mother with the rod in her hand.

"Evah sence yo' bin in dis gap yo' been pickin' 'pon me. Why yo' don' le' me an' me chirrun alone, ni?"

"Well, why yo' don't tell dem not to extafay wit' mine, den, no? Tell dem de little watahmout' runts, not to come on my hedge-row an' pick an' mo' o' my tam'rin's. Oi'll set poison fo' dem, too. Why yo' don't feed dem? Why yo' don't giv' dem a good stiff ball o' cookoo so dat dey won't hav' to teef my tamarin's? Pack o' starved-out runts!"

"Who is any starved-out runt?"

"Yo'! Who yo' t'ink Oi is talkin' to, but yo'?"

"Yo' nasty t'ing yo'!"

"Yo' murrah!"

"Bad-minded wretch!"

"Call me all de bad-minded wretch yo' like but Oi betcha yo' don't hit mah!"

"Oi don't hav' to low-rate myself fi' suit any field han' neygah uman like yo'."

"Hey," laughed Zink Diggs, her arms akimbo, "hey, anybody hear she talkin' would 'a' t'ink she is the Queen of England!"

"Come, Alfie, le' we go an' leave de wretch!"

IV

At serene peace with the Lord, April was sent one dusk, the reddish tints of a Barbadian twilight spreading a lovely fervor over the land, into a spasm of alarm.

"Hey, Miss Emptage—"

A high-pitched neighbor's voice rose above the music of the wind humming over the cane piece.

"Wha'm is, negh?"

"Zink Diggs tek up yo' goat."

"Pig!"

"Go quick befo' she chop awf she head."

"Run, mahmie—"

Chasing through the corn April went to the end of the boundary line, just in time to see Zink Diggs tethering the goat. She was singing and an air of joyous conquest was about her.

"Giv' me my goat," said April.

"Come an' tek she," said the other, pointing the reins at her. "Come an' tek she, ni, if yo' t'ink yo' is de uman Oi is dam well sure yo' ent."

"Always jookin' yo' han' in yo' matty saucepan," cried April.

"Wha' dah yo' say?" she cried, bewildered.

"Gypsy t'ing!"

"Wha' dah yo' say!" she cried, enraged. "Why yo' don't talk plain so dat a body can understan' yo'? Why yo' ha' fi' fall back 'pon dah gibberish unna tahlk dey whe' unna come from."

"Giv' me my goat," said April, "dat is ahl ah ax yo'."

"Dey she is," repeated Zink Diggs, pointing to Zenona. "Go tek she, ni!" But the goat was safely on Zink Diggs' ground.

April made a step to cross it.

"If yo' put a foot 'pon my sorrel I'll brek um fo' yo'," she murmured, vengefully.

"How much yo' wan' fo' de goat?" asked April at last.

"A shillin', an' yo' bettah be bleddy well quick 'bout it befo' ah carry de starved-out t'ing 'ome an' mek currie outa she."

"Teefin' vagybon' yo'," said April, water seeping into her eyes.

"Call me all de bad name yo' lik', but yo' ent gwine get

dis goat back to-night till yo' fork up dat shillin'. Dey'll have to jump ovah my grave befo' dey'll get yo' hungry goat fuss."

She turned to one of the children. "Go in de lardah, Mirrie, an' reach up 'pon de ledge an' bring de dah shillin' Bay Rum giv' me yestiddy fo' de eggs." She sighed, for it was her last one.

The child sped through the bush—spindling legs leaving the brown earth—and in a jiffy was back with the piece of silver bright in her dirt-black palm.

"Hey," said April, taking it and leaning over the ripening sorrel, "hey, tek yo' old shillin' an' giv' me my goat."

Zink Diggs grew hysterical at her approach. "Don't come near mah," she said, her eyes rolling wildly. "Stan' whey yo' dey an' put de shillin' 'pon de groun'! Don' come near muh! An' tek yo' ole hungry goat along."

April took the goat and dropped the shilling on the ground.

"Yo' t'ink Oi gwine tek any'ting out o' yo' nasty han'?" she said. "Yo' put um 'pon de ground." But before she picked it up she went in her bosom and drew out a little salt sack. She sprinkled two or three pinches of it on the coin before she picked it up.

The sun came out again. The crops bristled, the birds were singing. Triangles of birds, blackbirds and peewits, swarmed to the fragrant fruit, gave music to the wind. Hummingbirds—doctor birds—buzzed at the mouths of alluring red flowers.

April, a calico bag swung around her waist, picking the pigeon peas planted on the hedge facing Zink Diggs' land, sang hosannahs to the Lord. . . .

An' Crown-un-un Him Lahd av ahl

As she went along husking them, shelling the peas, she was soon aware of some one burrowing in the nearby hedge, and whistling

> Donkey wahn wahtah, hole 'im Joe
> Donkey wahn wahtah, hole 'im Joe
> Hole 'im Joe, hole 'im Joe,
> Hole 'im Joe, don't let 'im go—
> Donkey wahn de wahtah, hole 'im Joe.

She readily recognized Zink Diggs, but hardly, the words that followed.

"Good mawnin', Miss Emptage."

Being a child of the Lord, April answered, "Good mawnin'." She continued singing a Sankey hymn, and shelling the peas.

"You're not a quarrelsome uman," she heard Zink Diggs say, "but you're dam side mo' determined than I am!"

But she went on, not turning her head, singing the Sankey hymn.

V

It was spring; spring in Barbadoes. For the dogs—evil omen. Grippe. Sickness. Across the flowing acreage the brindle pup took a post near the goat. Nearby Alfie, Mirrie, Ona and Din were twittering, "Come, doggie; come, doggie—" and giving the poor wretch parsley.

"Go back an' put de pot on de fiah," April shouted to Mirrie as she strode through the corn-patch. "Go back an' boil de pigeon peas."

"Oi wan' fi' come, too."

"Go down de stan' pipe an' get a bucket o' water an' mek yo' oven, den."

They left her, and she went madly down to the end of her ground. On the rim of her land she met Zink Diggs. "Wha' yo' doin' 'pon my groun'?" she said. "Yo' muss be mek a mistake, uman, yo' ent survey yo' ground right."

"Yo' t'ink so?" the other cried, "Now look yah, Miss Emptage, yo' bin' lookin' fo' trouble evah sence yo' move in dis gap, yo'—yes, yo'—an' yo' dam well know dat when yo' wuz plantin' dem peas an' corn yo' wuz trespassin' 'pon my groun'. Uman, yo' mus' be outa yo' senses."

With a rope of banana trash to tie up her skirt—up so high that her naked legs gleamed above the tops of her English patent leather boots which the Doctor had ordered her to wear as a cure for "big foot"—Zink strode swiftly through the patch, dragging up by their roots, cane, corn, peas, okra—April's plantings.

"Move outa my way, uman, befo' Oi tek his gravallah an' ram it down yo' belly! Don' mek me lose me head dis mawnin' yeh, Oi don' wan' fo' spend de res' o' my days in de lock-up fo' killing nobody."

No rock engine, smoothing a mountain road, no scythe, let loose on a field of ripened wheat, no herd of black cane cutters exposed to a crop, no saw, buzzing and zimming, could have outdone Zink Diggs' slaying and thrashing and beheading every bit of growing green. Flat, bare, she left it.

April was afraid to open her mouth. She stood by, dumb-founded, one hand at her throat.

Gleaming in triumph, Zink gathered her bill and grav-eller and paused before she went. "Look at she dough," she said, "she look like Jonah when de whale puke he up!" And she flounced through the orchard, singing *Hole 'Im Joe.*

"Ona, come yah, quick!"

"Yo' always boddering me, why yo' don't—"

"Come, yah, gal—gal, Oi call yo'!"

"Wha' do yo', ni?"

"Me wan' fi' show yo' somet'ing, gal."

"Wah'm is, ni?"

"De black pin is ketchin' de house afiah."

"Gahd! Go tell mahmie—"

"Wha' she is?"

"Roun' by de shed roof."

"Mirrie, come yah, an' see wha' Din do! Ketch de house afiah!"

"It ent me! It is de black pin burnin'—"

Down by the back of the breadfruit tree Alfie and Mir-rie were sitting close to each other—very close. They hated to be diverted by such silly inquisitiveness. Calm, unexcited, Mirrie was prodding the boy to do something to her. She had put it down on a matchbox, in edge, scrawly letters— one word—but it refused to stir Alfie's sluggish desire. The scent of something ripe and rich and edible—something to be tasted with the lore of the tropics deep in one's blood— something bare and big and immortal as the moon—com-pelling something—began to fill the air about the little boy. He secretly felt it surging in Mirrie, and something beat a tattoo in his temples. Upon him a certain mirage fell—sure, unerring.

"Wha' yo' two doin' heah?" shouted Din, coming up. "Hey, Oi gwine tell mah mahmie 'pon yo' two."

"Wha' yo' gwine tell she? Yo' mouthah!"

"Dat—"

"Mout' run jess lik' sick neygah behine."

"Dat what? Wha' yo' ketch me doin', yo' liad t'ing yo'? I ent doin' nutton. I was just showin' Alfie—"

"Mirrie!"

"Comin', mum!"

His tongue thick, heavy, Alfie rose. "Yo' girl chirrun, if unna don't behave unna self, Oi gwine tell unna mahmie 'pon unna, too. Wha' all yo' makin' all dis noise fo'?"

"De pin ketch de house afiah."

"Wha' pin?"

"Fomembah de black pin Zink Diggs giv' Alfie fo' he mahmie?"

"Hey, yes."

"Gal, shut up yo' mout', yo' too stupid, how kin a pin ketch de house afiah?"

"Wha' is dah smoke, den?"

"Run an' tell mahmie, quick."

Ona, Din, Alfie, Mirrie—the last one, dusting, aggrieved, thwarted—galloped past the shed roof round to the kitchen.

"Mahmie."

"Quick, de black pin is ketchin' de house afiah."

"Gyrl, yo're crazy."

Swiftly drying her hands, she sped around to the shed roof. A gust of smoke darted, on the crest of a wind, from the place where the deadly missile had been imprisoned.

Surely, it was burning—the black pin had fired the shed roof! Out April tugged it. Once more she held it trembling in the sun. A smoking black pin. Some demon chemical, some liquid, some fire-juice, had been soaked into it originally. *Obeah* juice. "But Oi gwine sick de Lord 'pon yo'," vowed April, tossing it upon a mound of fowl dung and wormy provisions scraped together in the yard, and set a bonfire to it all. The fire swallowed it up and the wind sent a balloon of gray-white smoke-puffs streaming over Zink Diggs' hedge.

It had speed, and energy, and a holy vitality—the smoke; for it kept on till it got to Zink Diggs' house and then it burst puffing into it. It had hot, red, bitter chemicals, the smoke of the pin, and Zink Diggs' reaction to them was instantaneous. The smoke blew by, taking life—animal, plant. The dog dropped, the leaves of tea bush she had picked and had on the kitchen table, withered suddenly. It left her petrified by the stove, the white clay pipe ghastly in her mouth. Even her eyes were left sprawling open, staring at the cat, likewise dead, by the smoking coal pot.

The White Snake

On the banks of a bilgy lamahau, the eeliest street-stream in Bordeaux, a row of Negro peasant lodgings warmly slept. It was a vile, backward crescent reeking in brats and fiendish lusts. *Cocabe* among its inkish rice-growers extended to gorillas sentenced to the dungeons of Surinam, Portuguese settlers who'd gone black, Chinks pauperized in the Georgetown fire of '05 and Calcutta coolies mixing *rotie* at dusk to the chorus of crickets and *crapeaux* moaning in the black watery gut.

The dawn rose a dewy crimson, and a blood-curdling sound polluted the vapory silences of a Negro lodging.

"Murdah! Police! Warlah! Hole 'im! Miss Ewin', tek'e arf me."

Fetid black snorers rolled restively, clawed, dug at bugs or itching veins rising bluely on bare, languid bodies, as if to say: *don't worry. It's nothing. Nothing but some Hindu coolie, after the evening's erotic debauch, to the roll of goat drums, outside, on the low lamahau earth, severing the head of some jewel-laden, thirteen-year-old mate, the third on a string of murdered conquests.*

But die the scream would not.

"Lahd—"

"Wha' de mattah wit' yo', gal? Why yo' don' let a po' body res'?"

"Tek it arf me, no—?"

"Tek wha' arf yo', gyrl, yo' mus' be crazy. Foolish t'ing! Tek arf yo' top lip!"

"Wahy—look he crawlin' up me legs! Quick, tek'e arf me!"

"Sahv yo' right. Tell yo' yo' eat too much hole pea soup 'n cawn meal dumplin'! Go 'long an' le' de mule ride up 'n down yo' belly."

"See 'im, dey! Dey he is! A white one—see 'im, Miss Ewin'? A white snake crawlin' up me foots—tek 'e 'way. Quick—o! Miss Ewin', Ah beg yo'! Help mah!"

"Gyrl, get up! Yo' only dreamin'! It ent no snake fo' true—get up. It's mawnin'. An' go down to de stan' pipe 'n bring up de bucket o' hossah yo' lef' out dey las' night—"

"O! Lahd, Oi wuz frighten so—"

"Yo' heah ne, ni, Seenie? An' don' fuhget to blow de kerosene lamp out befo' yo' go."

The whole thing seemed to follow as a natural sequence. For Jack Captain, a Berbice mulatto, was an energetic wooer.

And then one rosy dawn, a dozen Hindu fires kindling the lamahau, the gold-digging *macaume* lured from Seenie the seed of her all.

II

Outlawed by the sorrowing blacks of Bordeaux, Seenie, "to exculpate she wickedness," fled to Waakenam, a sparsely populated isle on the Essequibo Coast. There she took refuge in a hut deep in the Guiana woods. Until a lackey on the constable's staff had dubiously led her to it, the cabin was deserted, cane trash crowned it like a wreath of *callaloo* mist. Box square, inside it was dark and cloudy. The peon originally occupying it had evidently had a vivid contempt for the tropical sun or wind. And it was here that Seenie, hardly able to survive the social consequences of lust, felt happy in raising Water Spout.

Inside the hut, by way of a bit of color, Miss Esteena, the niece of the Negro head of the Waakenam constabulary, had given her an old canopied mahogany bed.

Into the boy's flower-like mouth she pried a spoon with the crusted refuse of the previous day's stewed cassava.

"Eat um, sah," she cried, "an' don't put on no 'ears, lik' yo' is any man. Eat um, Oi say."

Upon Water Spout's glazed tawny body there was not a stitch of clothes. But it was fiendish hot in the cane trash hut, and he needed none. His puny body, which the *obeah* midwife had despaired of so, had flecks of porridge, and hardened bread swobbed in tea, on it. He had a scrawny neck. It had its base in a hollow-sounding delta. A stack of bluey veins, loosely tied in a clot of skin, connecting a hairless cocoanut to a brown, belegged pumpkin. The naval string, prematurely plucked, hung like a ripe yellow cashew. Bandy, spindling legs jutted out, to either side, from beneath a rigidly upright little body.

As a sort of aftermath to a night of studied rest, Seenie was dizzy, drowsy but she made sure of one eternal thing—Water Spout had to be fed. Feeding him was her one active passion. It was the least, she felt, she could do by him. Her ways may have been bad, her soul in doubtful retrospect, but Water Spout had to eat—*hossah*, cane licker, green peas, anything. And, by Jove, she had plans for him: later on, it was her idea, no matter how austere Miss Esteena was, to let him go down to the river by himself. If she had anything to do with it, Water Spout would some day walk!

"Come, Water Spout, come play wit' mamma!" Somewhere, in the frowsy dark, she had seized a toy, a symbol of Miss Esteena's charity at Yuletide, and shaking it gave it to him.

Glazed-eyed, he reluctantly took it; he made no effort to wring joy and sound out of it.

As he grew older, she saw to it that he wasn't left by himself on the bed; not that she minded his wetting it, so that when she came home at night she had to take refuge on the floor, if she wished a dry spot to lie on. But time was slowly proving that there was life awake and raging in his glazed little body, which all along had seemed to her to lack virility. And he would, by the wreckage he'd leave behind, play, dance and roll—make noise!—in a fury of possession, with some jaunty toy wagon or cart horse she had given him to play with. No, it didn't pay to leave him up there on the bed. He might fall to the unkempt floor. Then, again, although he refused to cry, no matter how often or how hard he would fall, in some quiet, unobtrusive way, the idea began to enter Seenie's head that he might not do so well, after all, from all these constant falls and things. His refusal, his failure to cry, started in her queer trains of thought.

At first they excited a more unobservant severity.

"Yo' too stubborn, sah, yo' too mannish—look at he dough—he look lik' something dog no like."

"Yo' so little an' yo' so ownwayish," she'd say to him, "yo' won't cry, ni, yo' won't cry—well, Oi gwine show yo' somet'ing," and she'd beat him for fair.

All this, when, turning away his little head, he'd try to shove the spoon with the fluff of corn mash away from him; or after a bowl of cane juice, when, with only the warning of a writhing face, he would unbosom himself, abdominally speaking.

And then Seenie, with the instinct of a heifer, began to argue that after all there must be something wrong with Water Spout, with any child, as lavishly fed as he was, who didn't stamp and yell and knock things out of one's hands and dribble at the mouth and lather with spit everything he came in contact with—the little heathen!

"Behave like a good lil' boy yo' heah?" she said, a bit penitently, pausing at the door. She shook a chastising finger at him. "Behave yo'self, heah, an' yo' mahmie will bring yo' a sugar plum."

> Clap han' fuh mahmie
> Til pahpie come
> Bring sugah cake
> An' giv' Seenie some!

And she went out, slamming the door behind her.

The world of Seenie's flight was a terrible green. "Me baby chile," she murmured, "me own baby chile." The edge and sweep—wide and far-flung—of leaf and vine, shrub and

fruit, flower and sky; the tender flush of the river dawn—
brought a barbaric peace to her soul.

Snaky cords tightened in her brain. "Yo' mek up yo' bed,
now go lay down on it," Miss Ewing, the Bordeaux sorceress
had said to her. And with Captain, with whom the whole
thing was a dismal oversight, she had implored on bended
knees, to no Christian purpose, for having lost sight of, in a
heat of frenzied lust, the fruit of her innocent pride.

III

Coral earth paved the one flake of road in Waakenam. Gathering depth and moss, the water in the gutters beside it was
a metallic black. It was a perfumed dawn—the strong odor
of fruit and turpentine flavoring it. For it was high up on the
Guiana coast, and the wind blew music on the river. Vivid
flame it blew on the lips of grape and melon, and ripened, like
the lust of a heated love, the udders of spiced mangoes and
pears peeping through the luscious grove.

Now and then, by the grace of the rollicking wind, there
appeared in the dense forest the sparkle of resin hardening
on the bruised trunks of balata. Sometimes, where the water
in the gutter streamed, the music on the Essequibo touched
fruit and flower and resulted in a flurry of orchids floating on
to Calvary.

And in the distance, beyond the violent patches of green,
flowing to a reddish upland, smoke—the vapors of boiling
syrup—tarnished the white marl-gemmed sky.

On awakening on mornings Seenie indulged in a rite
native to the Negroes of the region. She'd slip on a one-piece

frock, and go outside to the rain water cask which had a zinc drain pouring off the cabin roof into it. There her toilet was done.

And as sure as the sun rose, there'd be on the dewy ground, on the boughs of mango and pine, lovely, quiescent, a gallant cordon of snakes. Now as she sped forward, the road shone with them. Gorgeously bedecked ones—two inches of blue, two of mauve, two of yellow—two of black. Some, the coral ones, a yard or more in length, lovely crown jewels. Green snakes, black snakes, reaching up to the shady bush and swamp—drowsy on the sandy road.

When she reached the constable's, a high wooden dwelling in ample view of the stream, Seenie took charge of the pantry. She tied on the ruffled bib, stuck a scornful nose in the larder, sampled skeptically the plantain, stewed in cocoa fat, which she had put aside the previous evening, following a tradition of the tropics, for any starving ghost who might pass along in the night.

"T'row de t'ing 'way, gal, um ent no good, um sour," she said, and heaved it through the window.

There were even limits to Water Spout's gastric feats.

Suddenly a fragrant presence invaded the pantry.

"Good morning, Seenie," said Miss Esteena.

"Mawnin,' mum," replied the girl, sticking a match under the chocolate kettle in the coal pot.

An illuminating contrast; the girl, grating the cassava for the *bake* the Sergeant liked so well; with her despairing uncomely face, the high cheek bones, the sprawling mouth eternally white at the ends, the tapering chin. On the other hand there was reflected in Miss Esteena's sullen grace the fruit of a Negro culture as old as the civilization of the Incas. An Albertown belle, she was tall, brown, beautiful. Shimmering in white, the collar of her hand-wrought bodice closed high about her throat after the fashion of the time of Mary Queen of Scots.

"Be sure," said Miss Esteena, in her sharp, pointed tones, "to season the corass, properly, Seenie. Put plenty of salt and pepper and steam it long and well with the pot half full of water. Until it begins to crack. Then call me."

"Yes, mum, when Oi get roun' to it, mum."

But Miss Esteena was used to help of her own hue, and so had come to shut her ears to the thin veil of obedience in the Bordeaux girl's voice.

Gathering up the hem of her skirt, she moved austerely from the rice, green in a dish on the vined sill, to the fresh shelled peas, the tray of soaking *cashews*, the sugary sour sop, under a wire cage away from the flies.

"You know, Seenie," she said, "when you get time I wish you'd plant some mustard seed over there in the garden. Look!"

"Yessum, Oi see—"

Grating cocoanut was a hazardous task. And it required a constant fluid motion. Grinding it till the skin became thin as a tip of flame, she had got her palm bruised, and blood spots spattered the white juicy nut.

She leaned over the window squeezing it.

"Under that tree," said Miss Esteena, "see where I mean?"

"Yo' mean—dey—yassum!"

"And perhaps you could stick in a few knots of cane and some pumpkins on the hedge."

"Passably some carrots, too, mum. But yo' won't want anyt'ing what gwine gaddah too much bush. Yo' fomembah wha' ole Hart say, he say too much grass will bring de snakes."

"There you go again, you and your snakes. Can't you think of anything else to be afraid of?"

"Fi' tell yo' de troot, mum—"

"Gracious me, are they digging again? Look—there—by the trench—Seenie, what are they digging?"

"Wha' mum?"

"Can't you see it, stupid? There! Are you blind?"

"Oh, yassum! Me taught yo' mean yondah, mum."

"You always think something contrary!"

"It are a grabe dem a dig, mum."

"A grave? Mercy! For whom? What sort of a grave is it?"

"Fo' de baboo wha' chop arf 'im wife head, mum," said Seenie.

"Oh, mercy!"

"Dem gwine hang 'im up dey an bury 'im under de scraffold dem a build dey. See it, mum? All dem board yo' see dem a pile up dey is fo' de scraffold dem gwine knock togaddah fi' hang 'im."

"Well, well, the idea!" exploded the constable's niece, pacing the pantry madly. "If it isn't one thing it is another. Yesterday, it was finding a snake coiled up under my writing table, foaming to strike. Last Tuesday, at the *soirée* on the Governor's visit to the colony, it was having a black camoodie secrete itself, the Lord only knows when and how in the chandelier and as soon as Lady Fordyce-Boyce and Captain Burt selected to hold their tête-à-tête underneath it, began to burrow into Lady Fordyce-Boyce's red hair.

"Now by Jove, it is to wake up and find them erecting under my very window a scaffold to wring the neck of some wife-killing Hindu. I have never heard the like of it in all my days."

"Dat a fac', mum," meekly murmured Seenie.

The missus strode out, raving. She was going herself to the Sergeant and ask to be shipped back to Georgetown at once.

"Cho," said Seenie, "she mek a fuss ovah nutton."

IV

The wind, alternately hissing and snarling, brought to Seenie's ears the roar of the Essequibo belching cargo on the wooded shores of Waakenam. O! Placid, godless wind! It brought heroic tales of Georgetown muck on a briny dash to the gold fields.

> Gold, Pataro gold
> O! de rich man
> An' de po' man.

O! intimate, loquacious wind! It told epic tales of black men, the salt of adventure seasoning the marrow in their bones, in *bateaux* (the flat-bottomed curses) speeding, nugget laden, down the *tacabah*-paved river—suddenly becoming songless!

> Ovah danger, danger, danger
> Danger, danger, danger, danger
> Rocks an' Fall—!

You Mistah *Tacabah!* A sea lion, a sea cow, a shark? No! Great big slices of timber fastened, growing in the river! Deep-rooted, they were animals—groveling in the bowels of the unsettled stream. And *Tacabah*, the perpendicular beast, had eyes and ears, feet and heads. And *Tacabah* could butt. On a starless night, he, the master of the river's fate, the hairy prowler of its incalculable depths, usually got on the war path. How easy it was for him! All a headlong *bateau*, oared by a lot of drunken gold diggers, need do was touch it—it was hardly necessary to jam it—and *Tacabah'd* get the laugh on *bateau!* Over it'd go—at *Tacabah's* jerky butt—heading for the eely monster's bowels, planted deep in the roots of eternity.

> Ovah danger, danger, danger,
> Danger, danger, danger, danger,
> Rocks an' Fall—!

The moon, rambling about in the torrid sky, now and then gleamed on something Seenie carried on her head. It was a skillet filled with soup. Dozens of Cayenne peppers, hot as the water blazing in an equatorial sea, had gone into its making. Only throats of the purest steel were able to give passage to it. It was ghastly stuff. Eating it at night, Seenie'd bring heat to bear on heat. After a draught she'd light the kerosene lamp, discard the chimney and open her mouth over the flames till her throat cooled. It was a rite rivaling the starkest *brujerial* act. In the skillet of red terra cotta, was Water Spout's portion of the flaming broth.

All the thwarted sounds of creation rose to a mighty murmur in the obscuring night. Deep in the thicket four-legged beasts stalked. There was baying. Sheep, torn by a species of wolf hounds on the Coast, remained silent. But the dogs were less cultivated, and there was deadlier tearing done.

Along the road iguana, the sparkle in their eyes jeweling the tropic night, pursued shy, petty quests. And from the hedge came the silken slither of snakes about to lather with foam and strike some legless sheep or ox left by the mutinous pack.

The words of a song sung by the peasants of the East Coast rose on Seenie's melodious lips:

> Minnie, Minnie, come yah!
> Salam-bo come yah!
> Salam-Matanja, come yah!
> Le' Quackah-Tanyah, 'tan' dey!

Abruptly she left the coral road and unerringly stopped, in spite of the branching of leaf, at the cabin rising a little ways in.

"Water Spout!" she shouted, entering.

A wave of heat flew up at her. It was cane trash, hot hut heat. Heat smelted in a furnace untouched by a gust of fresh wind.

She called, but only a stream of hot mist, making for the door, answered her. "Oh berry well," she cried, "'im sleep, po' fellah."

She went to the table on the lower side of the hut and drawing a match lit the lamp. Darts of light flitted to the dark corners of it. Once able to distinguish things, she turned, and spied him on the bed.

She went to him, candied words on her mouth. He was in a deep, moist spot. A hole, really, bored into the rotting mattress. Gently she lifted him up, and the light fell on his sleeping face.

She took him to the table, and forced some of the soup into his mouth. But seized by a sudden spasm of energy, he refused, and spat it up, with a gurgling accompaniment. Then he curled back to her, fumbling for the avenue to her breasts. But she laid him back on the bed, consoled that he'd wake up in the night, demanding to be nursed.

"Lahd, me tiad, sah," she cried, yawning and undressing.

Presently she blew out the light and crawled in the bed beside him.

V

O! sleep, soundless sleep!

The night gathered heat. The straw crackled and pricked. Once a board slipped to the floor.

But sleep!—endowed, concentrated!

Cycles of the day sped through Seenie's head. There was a fugitive line between them and the half realized happenings in a dream. It was a work cycle; not one of song. Cooking, washing, ironing. Peccadilloes. Scraps for Water Spout. Reining herself in, and not exploding at the golden rancor of Miss Esteena. Ready at any time to do for the Sergeant, a grave, white-templed man, who rose at dawn and retired at midnight. Saying but a word which kept his niece in talk for a week. Men drowning like rats on the Essequibo. The river a *tacabah* nest. The Sergeant's men, dying by the dozens, of fever—worms breeding in the unemptied casks set to catch rain water—bringing in *hossah, corass,* for her to scale and stew—and bring home to stuff in Water Spout's hardening belly! Ah, the pepper soup did that. It had, about a barrel of it, straightened his legs; but at the expense of his gums and his belly which were hard as rock.

Suddenly—a flashback to reality.

Water Spout had begun to cry. About time. Had she been dozing long? There was no one to tell. And he was hungry, and he cried.

"Come," she said, awaking, "come to mahmie, son." And she put out a hand in the dark for him. Ah—there—there he was. Crying. Cockling. She seized him by the neck, frontwards. It was moist, swobbled. A bit cold. She drew him to her, forcing the tip of a breast in his mouth.

From her a luxuriant warmth flowed out to him. And she dozed back again.

Dream horses riding her. The Cayenne soup no doubt; whereas usually she would be dead, dead to the fires of the earthiest hell.

Nibbling at her breast.

Gently tugging.

Sensation sweet—pumping milk in a black child's mouth!

Letting him pump it himself.

Doze. Dozing. Dreams—

Bordeaux. All the old figures resurrected to a distant reality. Old, shaky, fire-eating Miss Ewing. Captain; Berbice hermaphrodite. *Macaume!* Blacks, girls in particular, on the banks of the *lamahau,* at night talking about her. The baboos, behind pots of *rotie* and *callaloo*, beating on the back of a frying pan—

> Hack ba la la
> Hack ba la la
> Mahaica is comin' down!

The Hindu settlers begging for rain. Wouldn't the water in the *lamahau* do?

Staring at her, the very coolies. Wildly.

Miss Ewing, at last, late one night, getting a midwife to finger her. This way, then that. Sometimes she refused. And Miss Ewing, heartless, lavished boxes and clouts. Thumpings. And then free of one ordeal, another ensued. Urchins in the *lamahau* dusk slinging paining words at her. Swell belly Seenie. Swell belly—

> Jahn Belly, Quackah Belly,
> Swell like a cocoa

Her own swollen in time like a ripe jelly cocoanut. Aiming at the stars.

Soft tugging—

No? He was crying again.

Nonsense.

"Nevah min', son, com' to yo' mahmie." She was loving and awake. No, it couldn't be—something was wrong—he wasn't crying. Was she still dreaming? No! She was nursing the brat! Here—his cold head pegging at her armpit—here—tugging away at her very gizzard.

She began to feel for him. A soft, cool, flat something met her hand. His forehead, most likely. Sweat—was it that hot—or was he sick—the ague—fever—the rain water—crying—

Still he managed to be on the floor yelling. How was that? Was he a dual being?

Here he was at her breast, gnawing away at it. And there he was down on the floor, howling.

Absurd!

Again the exploring hand went out. Why, here he was, of course, the dual rascal, nursing! (Pity it was so blamed dark!) Certainly he was nursing. And she proceeded to make sure for the last time.

But suddenly the head receded, slipped down into the gut in the straw. And on the other side of the room Water Spout gave a loud unmistakable yell.

Jumping up, Seenie flew to the child and snatched him to her bosom, tight.

"Oh, me Gawd, me Gawd," she screamed, bursting through the door into the silence of the Guiana night.

It was barren sky. Frosts of dew, flakes of sunlight, fell upon the earth, fell likewise on the black gleaming uniform of one of the Sergeant's men, unhurriedly making for the hut.

Some six hours later he returned, dragging on the coral road to the sea the fresh dead body of a bloaty milk-fed snake the sheen of a moon in May.

The Vampire Bat

He was one of the island's few plantation owners and a solid pillar of the Crown. He had gone forth at the King's trumpet call to buck the Boer's hairy anger. But at last the guerilla warrior had become a glorious ghost and the jaunty buckras were trekking back to Barbadoes.

Flying into a breastwork of foam, the English torpedo boat had suddenly stopped, wedged in a sargasso reef a dozen miles from the Caribbean sea. After landing at a remote corner on the jungle coast, Bellon was forced to make the trip, a twelve-mile affair, on drays and mule carts over the brown, hoof-caked road to Mount Tabor.

But Mount Tabor, once a star on a pinnacle of wooded earth, was lost to old Sharon Prout's Boer-fighting son.

Wrecked in the storm which swept the island the very week Bellon had embarked for South Africa—it was a garden of lustrous desolation. Weedy growth overspread it. The lichened caverns below the stoke hole, once giving berth to hills of cane husk—fodder for the zooming fire—fertilized beds of purple beans. A stable, housing a mare and landau, stood on the old mill's bank. Rows of *taches*—troughs into which the cane's juice was boiled and brewed through a succession of stages until it became a quarry of loaf sugar—

frothed green on the rich, muggy land. One was a pond. Frogs and green water lilies floated on it. Another, filled to the maw, gave fathomless earth to breadfruit.

The old shaggy mare, a relic of the refining era at Mount Tabor, plodded through the dead, thick marl. Wearing a cork hat and a cricketer's white flannel shirt, open at the throat, Bellon drew near the woods to Airy Hill.

He trotted down a slanting road in to Locust Hall. A mulatto cane cutter, poxy progenitor of twenty-one husky mule-driving sons, stood under the raised portcullis, talking to a woman. Pulling at a murky clay pipe he was slyly coaxing her to a spot in the cane piece. His juice-moist bill, bright as a piece of steel, shone in the fern-cluttered gut. Blacks on sluggish bateared asses mounted the hill mouthing hymns to drive away the evil spirits.

> Father, O Father
> . . . past the fading rays of night
> Awake! awake!

Game-vending squatters streamed down from Flat Rock, cocks gleaming on trays which saddled their heads. From the shining hills the estate's night hands meandered in, pecking at greasy skillets. Corn meal flecked the snowy marl.

Reminiscently Bellon ruffled the horse's mane. "You old war horse, you." Once, long before the storm, the blacks at Arise, one of the old man's estates—a stark, neurotic lot— had burned and pilfered the old sugar mill, while the buckras were confabbing on the seashore of Hastings. Rayside, then but a frisky colt, smelling a rat, had made a wild dash for the city—neighing the tidings to the buckras.

Now it fell to the young heir to be returning to Waterford, the last of the old man's estates, on the back of the heroic old mare.

It was ten o'clock at night and he had yet fourteen miles to go.

A lone moon-swept cabin or a smoker's pipe light, blazing in the canes, occasionally broke the drab expanse of night. The road trickled on, deepening into a gully. There rose above it rocky hedges, seeding flower and fruit. Swaying in the wind, the cane brake grew denser, darker. The marl lost its prickly edge and buried the animal's hoofs in soft, gray flour. Laboriously she loped through it.

The road gently lifted. It perceptibly dazzled the myopic beast. The marl returned. It blazed white, and shone. The earth about it seemed bare and flat and the cane brakes thinner. And the moon hung lower. A rickety donkey cart suddenly came jogging down the hill. A creole woman, atop an ass, trotted by. The wind soared to a higher, sturdier level. It blew like breezes on the gay Caribbean sea. Had it been noon, or dusk, blackbirds would have speckled the corn fields or sped low above the reeling canes. But the moon ribbed the night and gave the canes, tottering on the high flat earth, a crystal cloaking.

Now the road faltered, steadied, and as the road slanted, the marl thickened until it became flour dust again. The cottages at The Turning hove into view.

"At last," the captain cried, and the lanky mare quickened at the proximity of feed. Her reins fell on her back, limp with sweat.

Opposite a Negro baker shop Bellon dismounted, hitched the animal to a guava tree, and knocked upon the door.

"Who dat?" shouted a voice from within.

"Captain Prout," he replied, and the door swung to.

Squat and stout, Mother Cragwell, a Ba'bajan creole—mixture of white and Negro—admitted him, and shuffled back behind the counter, eying the visitor. She had been kneading dough, the counter was lathered with it, and her hands were scaly with shreds of flour.

"Mas' Prout," the old woman exclaimed, wha' yo' a do down yah dis time o' night? Yo' na'h go home no?"

"Why, yes, Mother Cragwell," replied the officer jovially, "can't a law-abiding colonist walk the King's highway after dark?"

"De King's highways," the old woman sarcastically muttered, "Wha' dey care 'bout any King?"

Fixing her brownish-red eyes on the buckra, she looked puzzled, skeptical.

"Why, is that the sort of welcome you give a returning soldier, Mother Cragwell?" he inquired, flattered by the old woman's characteristically racial concern.

She shook her head, ruefully bestirring herself. "Han' me dat bucket dey," she said. "How much yo' want?"

"Oh, fill it," he said, fetching the pail, "the road is beginning to tell on the old wretch."

"'Bout time," murmured Miss Cragwell, who'd been a fixture at The Turning for over thirty years.

She half-filled the pail with molasses, burst a bag of flour into it and began mixing the mash with a ladle.

"Well, I suppose this is her last trip to Waterford—she's entitled to a pension for the rest of her life, the horny old nag."

He took the mare the foaming mash and returned to be

confronted by a cup of chocolate, a knot of burnt cane and a tasty banana tart. Among bill-twirlers, mule-cart drivers, and cork-hatted overseers and estate owners, Mother Cragwell's "drops" and sweet bread, turnovers and cassava pone, were famous to the farthest ends of the Ba'bajan compass.

He cordially sat down to the mulatto's informal hospitality. "I knew," he observed, "that I'd have to wait till I reached The Turning before I could prove I was back in the colony." He took a relishing sip and the old creole's glare fell.

"Mas' Prout," she said, "Yo' bes' don't go down de gully to-night, yo' hear?"

"Why, what's happening in the gully, Mother Cragwell?" he smiled, splitting the sugar cane. "Is the man in the canes prowling about? Or do you think the duppies will be haunting Rayside's tracks?"

But the young Briton's banter chilled the old mulattress. "If yo' know what is good fo' yo'self, yo' bes' hear wha' Oi tell yo'," was all she said.

"H'm! this tastes like good old West Indian rum!" he cried, taking another fig of the cane. "Did you burn it yourself, Mother Cragwell?"

"Who, me? No, bo," she retorted, looking up. "Dah cane yo' got dey come from down de road."

"What, did they have a fire there recently?"

"Yes, bo. Las' night. The fire hags ketch it fire las' night."

"The who?"

"Hey," the old woman drawled, shocked at the young man's density. "Hey, look at his boy, ni. Yo' don't fomembah wha' a fire hag is, no? An' he say he gwine down de gully to-night."

Bellon burst into a fit of ridiculing laughter. "Why, shame upon you, Mother Cragwell!"

"Ent yo' got piece o' de ve'y cane in yo' mout' suckin'?" she cried, fazed, hurt.

"Tommyrot! Some jealous squatter fired the brake, that's all."

"Yo' believe dat?" challenged the old lady, "Orright den, go 'long. Go 'long, bo. All yo' buckras t'ink unna know mo' dan we neygahs. Go 'long down de gully 'bout yo' business, bo."

He rose, handed her a shilling and started for the door.

Suddenly a whinny from the mare—a wild scream in the night—startled him.

"Who dat?" shouted Mother Cragwell, seizing an old cricket bat and going towards the door.

"Oh, me Gard, me Gard, me Gard—"

The door was slapped open and a Negro woman, draped in white, shaking a black parasol and a hand bag, entered. She was shivering and white-eyed and breathless.

"Calm yo'self, girl, an' stop wringin' yo' hands. Yo' gwine poke out a body eye wit' dat parasol yo' flo'ish dey."

"Oh, Miss Cragwell, Miss Cragwell—"

"Hey, sit down, Lizzie. It is Lizzie Coates. Wha' yo' doin' up yah dis time o' night, girl?"

"Oh, de man in de canes, de man in de canes—"

"Wha' he do to yo'?"

"Oh, de man in de canes, de man in—"

"Stop cryin' yo' big able goat 'n let a body see what's de mattah wit' yo'," frowned Miss Cragwell; she turned to Bellon. "Go behind de counter," she said, "an' like a good boy hand me de candle grease yo' see dey 'pon me chest o' draws."

"Oh, nutton ain't do me—he ain't do me nutton."

"Hey, yo' hear dis alarmer, ni," drawled Mother Cragwell, her lower lip hanging. "Wha' yo' mekin' all dis noise fo' den?"

A look of revulsion shone on Bellon's face as he returned. "God, she's black!"

"Oh, Mother Cragwell," the woman pleaded, dropping into a seat, "le' me tell yo'—"

Every word she uttered was punctuated with jabs of the inevitable parasol. "The light fool me," she said. "It was so light I bin taught it wuz morning."

"Yo' mean to say a big able woman like yo' ain't got a clock in yo' house?"

With difficulty the buckra kept back an oath of amused disgust.

"The light fool me, Ah tell yo'—"

"Yo' got a watch, Mas' Prout, wha' time it are?" asked Mother Cragwell.

He shifted his body to the other side. "Quarter to twelve," he said.

"Hey, it ent even twelve o'clock yet," breathed the black sweating woman, "an' here I wuz startin' fo' walk to St. Georges. I musta wuz drunk, an', gal, jess as I tu'n de corner—"

"Wha' corner?"

"Codrington Corner. By the wall. You know—down dey—"

"Ah'm."

"Who should I see standin' up 'gainst dey but a man."

"Lahd, tek me!"

"A man, gal, a man!" She fanned her black eagle face, the sweat brilliant on it.

"Wuz he alone?"

"Yes, ni."

"An' nobody wuz 'pon de road?"

"Not a blind soul gwine up or comin' down! An' me by meself mekin' fo' Waterford Bottom!"

"Gal, wha' yo' a do? Try fo' be a buckra?" And she cast an accusing eye at the white man.

A slow chuckle escaped Bellon as he tapped on his leggings with a black sage switch.

"Soul, I wuz so frighten I couldn't swallow good. I nearly choke, yes. But anyway I had my trus' in de Lord—

"Fust I taught it wuz a duppy—one o' de mans in de canes come back fo' haunt de po' neygah."

"Dey do dat," agreed Mother Cragwell, irrelevantly.

"Well, soul, when I mek de gap fo' tu'n into de gulley somet'ing tell me fo' change me umbrella from my lef' han' into my right an' my bag from my right into my lef'."

"Whe' wuz de man all dis time?"

"I put he out o' me taughts, girl. I wuzn't t'inkin' 'bout he. I had my mind 'pon de Lord an' de goodness o' His wuks—"

"Wha' a foolish ole goat yo' is! Why, girl, I su'prize at you! Wha', you ain't know any bettah? Wha' de man in de canes got fo' do wit' de Lawd? He don't care nutton' 'bout he!"

"Well, anyway, when I got down in de gulley it wuz so quiet yo' could heah de mongoose runnin' in de canes. It wuz so dahk yo' couldn't see yo' own hand."

"Hey . . ."

"Den I mek out anudder man comin' down de road . . ."

"Me po' Lizzie."

"Down de road. He wuz lightin' he pipe an' walkin' fast."

"Did he see yo'?"

"No, I don't t'ink he see me, but I could see he, dough, an' just ez I get up to he, I move one side fo' let he pass. An' soul just ez I got out o' he way, he bump right into somebody walkin' behind me!"

"Gard!"

"De man behine me wuz followin' me, gal, dah's wha' it wuz. Followin' me all dis time an' dere I wuz wouldn't knowin' it!"

"Yo' lucky, yes."

"Gal, I'm lucky fo' true! Soul, he bump into de man so ha'd de man even bu'n he mout' wit' de matches."

"An' wha' he do, buss he mout'?"

"De man comin' down de hill ax he pardin, but, soul, yo' should o' hear how he cuss he! 'Why yo' don't look where yo' gwine,' he shout out, 'yo' t'ink yo' own de road, no?'"

"An' wha' de man say to he?"

"Oh, de man only ax he pardin, an' went 'long 'bout he business."

"Why didn't he look whey he wuz goin'—"

"Shucks, he wuz so bent 'pon wha' he wuz gwine do he couldn't hav' eyes fo' nobody but me! An' de man humbug he object, dat's all. But wait, le' me tell yo'. Dah happen down in de gully. An' I went long, ent eben t'inkin' 'bout no man—"

"Ah tell all you' Seven Day 'Ventists unna is a pack o' nanny goats—"

"When all uva suggen somebody from behind put two long greasy arms roun' me neck, like he wan' fo' hug me!"

"De Lord hav' mercy!"

"Gal, I wuz so frighten I tek me umbrella an' I jerk it back ovah my lef' shoulder so ha'd de muscles still a hu't me!"

"Go 'way!"

"Jook! Straight in he eye—"

"Murdah!"

"Deed I did! Wha' business he ha' puttin' he ole nasty claws roun' me!"

"An' what he do, ni?"

"Gal, he le' me go so fas' yo' would'a't'ink de lightnin' strike he! An' I wuz so frighten I tu'n roun' ready fo' hollow fo' blue murder, but de Lord was wit' me an' He protect me. Fo' girl, he wen' runnin' in de gutter, pickin' up stones an' shying them at me."

"De wutliss whelp—"

"But girl, like I wuz heah, he was firin' dem ovah yondah! 'Yo' brute,' he say, 'yo' whelp, yo' wan' to jook out my eye, no! Yo' wan' to mek me blind, no!' An' all de time he was peltin' an' peltin' de rock stones at somebody a mile f'um me!"

"Yo' musta jook he in he eye—"

"Chile, if it wuzn't fo' dis umbrella I wouldn't know where I'd be by now. It's de Lord's own staff o' life."

With a piercing chuckle the buckra walked to the door. "Well," he drawled, "I guess I'd better be going. It's getting late."

Abruptly Mother Cragwell rose and went to him. "Yo' still gwine down de gully, son?" she begged, half-tearfully.

"Oh, don't be sentimental, Mother Cragwell," he said, with good-humor. "I'll manage somehow."

"Orright, bo," she shrugged, helplessly, "I can't say any mo' to yo'," and he went forth, loftily.

The mare took the road at a jog and a trot, till the huts grew dim, the canes and the hedges bushy. The moon was buried in a lake of blue mist and the marl ate into the animal's hoofs.

The Negro woman's tale excited a magic concern in the buckra.

There was a road opposite the baker shop which led through a dismantled estate, providing a short cut to Waterford. But Bellon remembered that it led over a steep gulley range—a tunnel a mile deep—a rattling river when it rained or stormed—now a rocky cave harboring wild dogs and lame mules, tusky boars and other, mystic finds.

He evaded it—the old Negress' tale ringing in his ears.

Somber, ruthless—the marl. The mare pawed and sieved it, stones soared topwards.

The moon burned the mist. It burned it away, leaving but a white crest of flame fire.

Suddenly, over the earth of gentle winds and sugar canes, balls of crimson fire plagued the sky! Fire hags at night—St. Lucia sluts, *obeah*-ridden, shedding their skins and waltzing forth at night as sheep and goats, on errands of fiery vengeance. Sometimes, on returning, at the end of the eventful night, they would find their skins salted—by the enemy—and, unable to ease back into them, the wretches would inquire, "Skin, skin yo' no know me?" And for the balance of their thwarted lives they'd go about, half-slave, half-free, muttering: "Skin yo' no know me, Skin yo' no know me?"

A bright-spirited party of Negro farm folk wrestling up the hill on basket-laden mules, came into view.

"Howdy, Massa."

"God bless yo', Massa."

"Gwine town, Massa?"

"Be ca'ful—de fire hag dem a prowl 'bout yah, Massa."

He pulled up the horse, puzzled at the spreading of the squirting fire.

"God—fire hags—surely the niggers can't be right."

He turned ashen, the reins in his hands tight, the horse pawing and pegging the marl understandingly.

The balls of fire subsided, but he was deep in the marl gully and unable to trace the origin of the pink hazes bursting on the sky's crest. The wind, however, was a pure carrier of smell, and the tainted odor of burnt cane filled the road.

"Wonder whose canes they're burning—"

Burning cane—the sky reflecting the distant glow— casks of rum boiling to waste at the will of some illiterate field hand!

He shouted to the animal.

"Giddup, horse!"

His head went swirling—the temptation to relapse conquered—barbaric *obeah* images filled his buckra consciousness.

Sugar canes burning—men in the canes—fire hags— nigger corpses—

Perspiration salted Bellon's brow.

Nigger corpses—nigger corpses—

And a legend, rooted deep in the tropic earth, passed pell-mell before him.

It concerned a river, a river red as burning copper and peopled by barques and brigantines, manned by blacks wedded to the *obeah*.

Once, the master of a vessel, taking a cargo of dry cocoanuts to a mulatto merchant on the other side of the coast, cheated; a few English crowns were at stake. But the trader was a high-priest of the *obeah*, and was silently aware of it. Forthwith he proceeded to invoke the magic of the *obeah* against the vessel.

At late dusk the returning vessel hoisted anchor. The festival rites, incident to her voyage, had drawn to the wharf, selling mango and grape, the mulatto courtesans of the river town. And the crew rained on them silver and gold, and bartered till the sun went down.

Upon reaching the vessel's deck the crew—the wine of lust red on their lips—grew noisy and gay at the sinking of the river sun. From below they brought a cask of rum, part of the cheated trader's store, and drank of it. With a calabash they dipped and wallowed in it, finding it sweeter than falernum.

Stars bedecked the night and a torch was lit. The vessel rocked on, falling in with the trade winds.

The rum was a siren, it led one on. The cask was deep, immense, but the liquor shrank till the huskiest of the Islanders had to be pummeled to lean over into it and dip the liquid out. With a score of itching throats there was a limit to the cask's largess, and the bottom was early plumbed. When they got to it, however, it was to find a rum soaked Negro corpse doubled up in the bottom!

The horse came to a dead, rigid stop. It was death dark and they had just entered the heart of the marl gully.

He was already fidgety, and grew urgent. "Come on, Rayside," he shouted, "giddup." But the mare shook, stamped, shuddered.

He stroked her mane, but a strange strong-headedness took hold of her. She flung her ears forward.

Bellon dismounted, and the mare's inelegant tail switched her bony flanks. He coaxed and patted her, but all she did was jerk her head the more.

Resorting to a flashlight, Bellon clicked it at her feet.

As the glare hit the marl, he recoiled, as one struck, at the spectacle it revealed—a little Negro baby sleeping in the marl!

"God, what's next!"—

Hesitatingly he approached, discerning that it lived, and moved.

For a spell he gazed at it, half-afraid. But for a diaper of green leaves it was nude. Then it occurred to him to pick it up.

Instantly the child reacted to its contact with human warmth and snuggled to Bellon's bosom. He smoothed its soft, bronze skin and the waif, with hands flagrantly like a bird's claws, burrowed closer to him.

With the child held close the buckra started for the horse, but—like a shot—Rayside bolted!

"Steady, mare!" Bellon growled, quietly reining her back in, "Easy, horse!"

One ear pasted flat on her mane, she stood impatiently still while he reached for the chamois blanket and swaddled the Negro baby in it.

Only then was he able to remount her.

Another of the colony's lurking evils, the desertion—often the murder of illegitimate Negro babes.

O God—another of the island's depraved nigger curses!

All the way up the hill Rayside reared and trotted, kicked and pranced, keeping to the edge of the marl road.

And the Negro waif's bird-like claws dug deeper into the buckra's shirt bosom.

He rode up the hill's moon-white crest until the shadow of Waterford fell upon him. He was tired, his brain fagged, his legs sore, his nerves on edge.

On the brink of a rocky hill extending beyond the estate stood a buckra overseer's cabin. Here Bellon's journey ended. He stabled the mare in the shed, glad to be rid of her. "Why, you don't even give me a chance to be temperamental—"

He took the Negro child in the cabin, angry at the physical proximity of it. "If any one had told me three weeks ago that after dodging Boer-shot I'd next be mothering a deserted nigger ragamuffin at two o'clock in the morning on a West Indian country road, I'd certainly have called him a God damned liar!"

He found a spot on the floor and brusquely cushioned the burden in it.

He was edgy, unstrung; he could not sleep. He tossed, half-awake, tortured by the night's fairy-like happenings.

As a boy at Arise the old man'd tell of fresh-born Negro babes dropped in eely wells in remote parts of the plantation jungle or wrapped in crocus bags and left in the canes for some ferocious sow to gnaw or rout.

Rapacious Negro ghosts—"men in the canes"—ha! ha! preying upon the fears of the uncivilized blacks.

Fire hags! St. Lucia mulatto sluts—changing their skins—turning to goats—sheep—prowling—going forth—

And weirdly interchangeable—Black Negro babes and vampire bats!

All night the fussy mare, with glassy eyes glued on the buckra hut, refused to touch corn or oats—stamping, kicking, growing uneasy.

The glory of the morning sun neared the cane hills. It burned past the mare's shed, leaving the animal still nervously gazing out it.

Inside the hut there sprawled the dead body of Bellon Prout. With a perforation pecked in its forehead, it was utterly white and bloodless.

On the ground the chamois blanket was curiously empty.

Coming up the hill the mulatto *obeah* girl who tidied the overseer's hut felt deeply exultant. For she was strangely conscious of the fact—by the crystal glow of the sun, perhaps—that a vampire bat, with its blood-sucking passion, had passed there in the night.

Tropic Death

I

The little boy was overwhelmed at being suddenly projected into a world of such fluid activity. He was standing on the old bale and cask strewn quay at Bridgetown watching a police launch carry a load of Negro country folk out to a British packet smoking blackly in the bay.

He was a dainty little boy, about eight years of age. He wore a white stiff jumper jacket, the starch on it so hard and shiny it was ready to squeak; shiny blue-velvet pants, very tight and very short—a little above his carefully oiled knees; a brownish green bow tie, bright as a cluster of dewy crotons; an Eton collar, an English sailor hat, with an elastic band so tight it threatened to dig a gutter in the lad's bright brown cheeks.

He was alone and strangely aware of the life bubbling around Nelson's Square. Under the statue masses of country blacks had come, drinking in the slow draughts of wind struggling up from the sea. City urchins, who thrived on pilfering sewers or ridding the streets of cow dung which they marketed as manure; beggars, black street corner fixtures, their bodies limp and juicy with the scourge of elephantiasis; cork-legged wayfarers, straw hats on their bowed crinkly heads; one-legged old black women vending cane juice and hot sauce.

It was noon and they had come, like camels to an oasis, to guzzle Maube or rummage the bags of coppers, untie their headkerchiefs, arrange their toilet and sprawl, snore, till the sun spent its crystal wrath and dropped behind the dark hulk of the sugar refineries to the western tip of the sky. Then it was their custom to pack up and sally forth, on the singing jaunt to the country.

Scores of ragged black boys, Gerald's size and over, filled the Square, half-covered by the dust, snoring. Old boys, young boys, big boys, little boys; boys who'd stolen on the wharves at sundown and bored big holes in the wet sacks of brown sugar; boys who'd defied the cops, and the sun, and the foaming mules, or the ungodly long whip of the driver, and skimmed on to tin cups the thick brackish froth the heat had sent fomenting up through the cracks in the molasses casks; boys who'd been sent to the Island jail for firing touch bams at birds lost in the bewildering city or for flipping pea-loaded popguns at the black, cork-hatted police.

Melting target for the roaring sun, the boy turned and gazed at the sea. It was angry, tumultuous. To the left of him there rose the cobwebbed arch of a bridge. Under it the water lay dark and gleaming. Against its opaque sides there were scows, barges, oil tankers. Zutting motor boats, water police-men, brought commotion to the sea. Far out, where the sun kissed it, the sea shone like a sheet of blazing zinc.

Creeping to the edge of the quay, he peeped over and saw a school of black boys splashing in the water. They were div-ing for coppers flung by black tourists on the side lines. They slept on the Congo-slippery rafts holding up the city, and would, for a ha'penny, dart after parasols or kites—that is, if the kites happened to be made of hard glazy "B'bados kite papah"—lost on the rolling bronze sea.

"Come, Gerald, eat this."

He turned and there was his mother. His big bright eyes widened for her. And a lump rose in his throat. He wanted to hug, kiss her. With the heat of his mouth he wanted to brush away her tears, abolish her sorrow. He wanted, too, to breathe the lovely, holy beauty of her.

"Come, son, tek yo' fingah outa yo' mout', quick, de launch will be yah any minute now."

He took the lozenge, the sun making it soft and sticky.

"Don't yo' want some ginger beer, son?"

"Oh, mama, look!"

The launch had come up, and one of the sailor-cops, a husky, black fellow, was making it fast.

"Orright lady, yo' is de nex'—come ahlong."

With much agitation she got in the boat. She had to hang on to her bag, to Gerald, and she was not prepared to get the ends of her slip wet. The men seized him, and she stepped down, barely escaping a carelessly dangling oar.

Bewildered, they clung to each other. "All right, son?" she said. But he was too unspeakingly concerned over the concurrent miracles of sea and sky.

Leaping through the sea, the boat would drown them in a shower of spray every time it came up, and Gerald was repeatedly tempted to put his hand in the water. "Keep yo' hands inside, sah," she cried, "shark will get you, too."

He remained aware of only foam and water, and the

boat's spit and sputter, and the warmth of Sarah's bosom. Away back, on the brown and gold of the horizon, he saw speeding into nothingness the scows and warehouses and the low lofts of Bridgetown. Now, the sea rose—higher, higher; zooming, zooming; bluer, darker—the sky, dizzier, dizzier; and in the heavens war was brewing—until the shroud of mist ahead parted and there rose on the crest of the sky the shining blue packet!

II

Sunday came. The sun baptized the sea. O tireless, sleepless sun! It burned and kissed things. It baked the ship into a loose, disjointed state. Only the brave hoarse breezes at dusk prevented it from leaving her so. It refused to keep things glued. It fried sores and baked bunions, browned and blackened faces, reddened and blistered eyes. It lured to the breast of the sea sleepy sharks ready to pounce upon prey.

Falling night buried the sun's wreckage. To the deckers below it brought the Bishop of the West Indies, a wordy, free-jointed man. He was a fat, bull-necked Scot with a tuft of red grizzly hair sticking up on his head and the low heavy jowl of a bulldog. He wore a black shiny robe which fell to the tips of his broad shiny black shoes. An obedient man, he had deserted the salon on the upper deck—deserted red-faced Britons in cork hats and crash on a jaunt to the iron mines of Peru—to take the Word of the Lord Jesus Christ to the black deckers below.

He very piously resisted grime and filth. On one occasion to avoid stepping on a woman's sleeping arm, he was obliged to duck under a hammock. It swayed gently and the man in it was one of those rare specimens—a close-mouthed, introspective Savanilla trader. As he shot up from beneath it, the Bishop was just in time to have splashed on the breast of his shining robe a mouthful of the trader's ill-timed spit. For half a second he blinked, and heated words died on his lips. But seeing the Colombian unaware of the impiety, he gruffly scrambled onward, brushing his coat.

Edging between a carpenter's awl and a bag of peas and yams, something ripped a hole in the Bishop's coat. He was sweating and crimson. His collar was too high and too tight. Stepping over a basin of vomit, he barely escaped mashing a baby. He was uncertain that he had not done so, and he swiftly returned and without saying a word gave the sea-sick mother half a florin.

He clapped a fatherly hand on Gerald's head, and the boy looked up at him with wondering bright eyes. Sarah Bright was sitting on the trunk skinning a tangerine.

"Your little boy?" smiled the Bishop, "smart-looking little chap, isn't he?" It was a relief to come upon them.

"Tu'n roun' yo' face, sah," she said, "an' lemme brush de sugah awf yo' mout'—" Assiduously she tidied him.

It was dark, and the ship was rolling unsettlingly. A kerosene torch spun a star-glow on the Bishop's pale tense face. He was about to address them. He was buried amongst a cargo of potatoes and the litter of the deckers. His was a sober impulse. On all sides the Dutch of Curaçao, the Latins of the Pass, the Africans of Jamaica and the Irish of Barbadoes—spat, rocked, dozed, crooned.

In a fetid mist odors rose. Sordid; tainted; poised like

a sinister vapor over the narrow expanse of deck. And with a passionate calm, the Bishop, clasping the Book of Books, faced them.

"O Lord, our God," he trembled, "O everlasting Father, again it is our privilege to come to Thee, asking Thy blessing and Thy mercy. Great God and Father! Thou knowest all things, Thou knowest the hearts of all men, and especially the hearts of these, Thy children! O Sacred Jehovah! purify their wretched souls—give unto them the strength of Thy wisdom and the glory of Thy power! Lead them, O Blessed Father, unto the pathway of righteousness that they may shine in the glory of Thy goodness! Help them, O! Divine Father! To see the light that shineth in the hearts of all men—we ask Thee Thy blessings in Thy son, Christ Jesus' name, Amen!"

III

Fish, lured onto the glimmering ends of loaded lines, raged in fruitless fury; tore, snarled gutturally, for release; bloodied patches of the hard blue sea; left crescents of gills on green and silvery hooks. Some, big and fat as young oxen, raved for miles on the shining blue sea, snapping and snarling acrobatically. For a stretch of days, the *Wellington* left behind a scarlet trail.

He was back in Black Rock; a dinky backward village; the gap rocky and grassy, the roads dusty and green-splashed; the marl, in the dry season, whirling blindly at you; the sickly fowls dying of the pip and the yaws; the dogs, a rowing, impotent lot; the crops of dry peas and cassava and tannias and eddoes, robbed, before they could feel the pulse of the sun, of their gum or juice; the goats, bred on some jealous tenant's cane shoots, or guided some silken black night down a planter's gully—and then only able to give a little bit of milk; the rain, a whimsical rarity. And then the joys, for a boy of eight—a dew-sprayed, toe-searching tramp at sunrise for "touched" fruit dropped in the night by the epicurean bats, almonds, mangoes, golden apples; dreaming of the day when the cocoanut tree planted at a particularly fecund part of the ground would grow big enough to bear fruit; waiting, in the flush of sowing time, for a cart loaded to the brim to roll rhythmically over the jarring stones and spill a potato or a yam. After silence had again settled over the gap, he'd furtively dash out on the road and seize it and roast it feverishly on a waiting fire; he'd pluck an ear of corn out of the heap his mother'd bring up from the patch to send to town, and roast it, and stuff it hot as it was in his tiny pants pocket and then suffer excruciating rheumatic pains in his leg days afterwards.

Usually on a hike to Bridgetown Sarah would stop at the Oxleys' on Westbury Road. Charlie Oxley was a half-brother of hers. Once he had the smallpox and the corrugations never left him. He was broad and full-bellied and no matter how hot it was he wore severe black serge. He was a potato broker, and a man of religious intelligence.

He had, by as many wives, two girls—and they were as lovely as fine spun silk. But Suttle Street, a pagan's retreat, was hardly a place for them so they were sent to Codrington to absorb the somber sanctity of the Moravian Mission. Now there came to crown the quiet manor on Westbury Road, another mistress, a pretty one, herself a mother of two crimson blown girls, *the quintessence of a spring mating.* They were a divine puzzle to Oxley. It was queer that their fathers, both firemen on a Bristol tramp, now blissfully ensconced in the heart of the Indian Ocean, had forgotten to return to tickle and fondle their pure white faces. . . .

It had happened in a peculiar way. And all through a silly love of song. Why did she ever encourage such a feeling? The legend of it was fast taking its place beside the parish's scandals of incest. Sea songs; songs sailor-men sang; ballads of the engine room and the stokehole; ditties fashioned out of the crusted sweat of firemen. Ah, it went beyond the lure of the moment. Bowing to it, she'd go, the lovely whelp, to wharf and deck when sunset was spreading a russet mist over the dusky delta of Barbadoes and give herself up to the beauty of song. Greedily songs go to the heart; go to the heart of women. It was bad enough being maid at a grog shop on a bawdy street and the upsquirt of a thundering Scot and an African maiden, but it was worse when the love of songs of the deep, led one at dusk, at dark, to descending stairs to stokeholes or to radiant night-walks on the spotless fringe of Hastings.

Mosquito one
Mosquito two
Mosquito jump in de ole man shoe.

At last, song-scorning, no more a slinger of ale, she had crawled, losing none of the primal passion she had formerly dazzled him with, over to Oxley's—to fatten on a succession of gorgeous nights of deep-sea singing and unquestionable sailoring.

Meditating on the joys attendant to the experience of seeing the Oxleys there came to little Gerald's mind the vision of soup. Rockhard crabs, tight-fisted dumplings, little red peppers, Cayenne peppers, used all to be in it. Sometimes there would be seasoning it with *hossah* or *corass* and parsley and white eddoes. And when they left, Mr. Oxley always gave Sarah a bag of potatoes to take home; but she was a lady and proud and it pained her to take it home on her head; but one of the neighbors, who had a donkey cart which came to town each day, would stop by and get it for her.

One forenoon when the sun was firing the hills of Black Rock, she had hurriedly decided to visit the Oxleys. To every one, down to the idiot Lynchee King, he of the maw worm, it was clear that something was tugging at Sarah Bright's throat.

To Gerald it was a quickening ordeal. All along the gap they went; up St. Stephen's Road—the birds brilliant-plumaged in the ripening cornfields—past the Gothic exterior of the Chapel to a steep decline where the hilly road was crowned by the falling leaves of a giant evergreen tree whose roots spread to every point of the compass. Up the road, the sun bright as a scimitar, the inexorable dust-marl heavy on them; past cow pens and meadows; past shops and cottages where folk inquisitively spied at them through half-shut jalousies. Then past the Mad House and Wolmer Lodge, a branch of the Plymouth Brethren, where Sarah "broke bread" and Gerald slept; up to Eagle Hall Corner and onward down to the roaring city. On the way he'd lift his piteous eyes to her sobbing face and implore, "Don't cry, mama, don't cry, God will provide for us."

At the Oxleys' the tension slackened. It was easing to be

there. They had a big, pretty house, plenty to eat, and the girls were lovely as the flowers whose fragrance was a dewy delight to the boy.

Again it was some sort of soup, fish soup, and the sensation of a hearty meal helped considerably to dissipate Gerald's concern over the things agitating his mother.

After dinner he and the girls, Vi and Rupertia, slid to the floor to play. A Bible was their toy. On their lips the letters of the word *contents* made a lascivious jingle. *Charlie open 'nen's t'ing ent nen's ting sweet.* Caught in their own impishness, they clapped their hands over their mouths, shutting off the laughter, and rocked against each other in riotous glee.

"Hey, Sarah, duh ought to lock he up, yes. Hey, you would 'a' t'ink a man wid fi' chirrun would ha' a bit o' conscience. W'en yo' say yo' hear from 'e las'?"

"June—le' mah see," snuffled Mrs. Bright, diving in her hand bag, "yes—it is June. June will be eight months sense Oi las' hear from 'e."

"An' yo' mean fo' tell muh," cried Mr. Oxley, his incredible eyes big and white, "dat dah neygah man ent ha' de graciousness in 'e 'art fuh sen' yo' a ha'penny fuh de chirrun awl dis time?"

"No, Charlie."

"Gord! Dah man muss be got de deart uv a brute!"

"He must be fuhget we, Charlie."

"Wuh, moy Gord, yo' don't even fuhget ah doig yo' fling a bone to, much mo' a big fambaly like yo' got dey. Fuhget yo'?"

"He must be," wept Mrs. Bright, swallowing hard, but Gerald was too impassioned himself to rise or let the girls share his sorrow.

"But wha' yo' gwine do, ni, Sarah? Wha' yuh gwine do? Yo' an' all dese chirrun yo' get dey, ni?"

"Oi ent stop fuh t'ink, Charlie, to tell yo' de troot. But de Lord will provide Charlie, Oi is get my truss in Him."

"But wha' kin de Lord do fo' yo' now yo' doan heah fum dat wooflees vargybin?"

"Ev'yt'ing wuks togeddah fuh dem dat truss in de Lorrd. Oi'll manage somehow. Oi'll scratch meself togeddah. De lil' bit o' money Oi get fum de house an' de piece o' lan' will jus' buy me an' Gerald ticket. Now all Oi is axin' yo' fo' do is put up de show money. Oi ent wan' no mo'. Dah is anuff. An' as de Lord is in heaven Oi'll pos' it back tuh yo' when the boat land at Colon."

"An' wuh yo' gwine do wit' de chirrun, ni, Sarah? Wuh yuh gwine do wit' dum?"

"Oi got Rosa fuh look aftah dem fo' me, bo. Yo' know Peony is wid she evah sense de holliduhs, an' she don't even wan' fuh come way, de ownway t'ing. But, yo' know, Charlie, Oi can't blame de chirrun, ni. Um ent nutton home fuh duh. Rosa is berry well satified fi' hav' she, aldo me can't say she ah happy riddance. No, not at all. Well, an de uddah gyrls, it gwine be ha'd 'pon dem, but Rosa house on Coloden Road is big enough fee tek cyah ah all uh dem, an' Mistah Foyrd only come home once a mont'. Rosa so lonesome, an' she so like de picknee dem. She will tek cyah uh dem fuh muh till Oi sen' back fuh dem. An' Oi only takin' Gerald wit' muh, po' fellah."

"Oi gotto go," she went on, in a hollow, dejected voice, "an' see wha' de mattah wit' Lucian. Oi can' go 'long tyin' mi guts no mo'. Oi too tired."

"Hey, but dah is a beast uv a man fuh yo', ni!" muttered Oxley in incredible outrage.

"Yo' know, sometimes Oi t'ink he muss be sick—"

"Sick?" he flew up, like a hen striking at a mongoose. "Dah man sick? Gyrl, hush up yuh mout'! Dah man sick? He ent sick no 'way! If he was sick doan yuh tink de nurse in de horspitral can write a letter even fuh a shillin' fuh he? Gyrl, go talk sense, ni! Dah man ent sick. He is jess a wufless stinkin' good fuh nutton vargybin' who ent learn fuh tek cyah uh he fambaly, dah is wuh he is! Oi tell yuh 'bout dese fancy mud-head men! Ent a blind one o' dem any blasted good! A pack o' rum-drinkin', skirt-chasin' scoundrels—dah's wuh duh is! Dey ort tuh lock he up, dey ort tuh get he 'n roast he behind fuh he—"

"Charlie!"

"Wha' Oi doin'? Ent um is de troot, ent um?"

"Oi ent gwine giv' up hope, Charlie, Oi still got my truss in de Lord."

"Yuh is ah bettah uman dan Oi is ah man, Oi know."

"If um is de will uh de Lord fuh me tuh suffer like dis, Oi is willin'. Didn't Christ die on Calvary's Cross tuh save yuh an' me an' Lucian—"

"Who, dat vargybun', don't put 'e 'long side o' me, Oi ent wan' none o' 'e nasty self fi' tetch me."

Some one intruded upon them. Sarah wiped away a tear. It was difficult to be there, denuding herself before that woman and her saucy girl children.

She came in, one of the girls at her side. "Hexcuse me, Charlie, but wuh yo' say, le' dem go?"

"Go weh?" he roared suddenly looking up.

"*To de fungshan*, no?" she replied, scornful of his brilliant memory.

"Cho," he said, turning back to Sarah, and staring at her searchingly, "All de time sochalizin', sochalizin'." He swiveled back round. "Ah say no! Yo' heah? No! Dem a stay in de house!"

"But it no a gineral saht o' shindig," she pleaded, "it a Miss Coaltrass dawtah what a hav' it."

"Ah don't giv' a dam pity hell who dawtah a hav' it—dem n'ah go!"

"But Charlie—don't!"

"Me don' mean fi' insult yo', Sarah, wit' me nasty tongue, but yo' mus' excuse me. But dese pahties dem 'nuf fi' mek Christ hesell bre'k loose."

"But me don't tink it are much—"

"Dem n'ah go—dat a sure t'ing! Could as well put it in yo' pipe an' smoke it! Saht'n fact! Dem tek up wit' too much gwine out orready. Wha' ah mo', dat Miss Persha, dem low-neck dress she ah wear, dem gwine giv' ar cold, too, yo' mahk an fi' mee wud."

"Wha' time it hav' let out, Persha?"

"Early, mam."

"Oh, le' de picknee dem go, Charlie, yo' too a'd on de gal chile dem."

"Dat's juss why me don't wan' dem fo' go. Awl yo' go out o' dis house at all howahs o' de night time, like unna is any umans, disregardin' whatevah awdahs dere is. Look at dat Miss Persha, she bin gwine out eve'y night dis week. Wha' she a go so? Wha' she a fine place fi' go so? But no mind; wait till me catch she, yo' wait."

"Dat a fac', Charlie, me hagree wit' yo' dey, me gwine put my foot down once an' far-all 'pon dem trampoosin's."

"Well, let de rascals dem go dis time."

IV

One day Gerald stole out on the deck. The sun was broiling hot. His mother was with him.

"Mama," he said, "let's go roun' de uddah side."

"Wha' fuh, sonny?"

"Ah wan' fuh go out dere at the Portugee shop an' buy a ball o' cookoo an' a piece o' salt fish. My mout' ain't got a bit o' taste."

"Yo' can't do that, son, there ain't any shops in the sea," she said, smiling weakly at him. "Come, let's go back—I don't feel so good."

Then it suddenly happened. They were below, it was dark, quiet, noiseless. Even the engines had stopped. Boom! it came. It sounded like the roar of a cannon. It shook the ship. Glass jingled. Things fell. Gerald's energetic mind flew hurriedly back to Black Rock. Often there would be sun and rain—all at once. The gap folk had become so used to it that they said it was the "devil and his wife fighting."

Until now lazy and half-asleep, the deckers rose, scrambling up on the above deck. Their baggage was going with them.

Gerald turned to his mother, busy combing her hair. She said, "Come, Gerald, put on yo' Sunday hat, son, yo' at Colon."

But he was skeptical. He stole upstairs and was an eager witness to the ship's surrender. The *Wellington*, a princess of the sea, had given in to the greater force of the earth. Soberly and serenely she had done so.

V

"Well, Sarah, who's this?"

"The last one, Gerald."

"He grow big, yes."

"Skipper don't even know he own son."

"Suck fingah buay."

"Shut up, Saboogles!"

"Fairf!"

"Come heah, son, don't cry—come 'n say howdee to yo' pappy."

"Tek yo' fingah outa yo' mout', sah."

"Say, something, no, Gerald—"

"Howdee!"

"Say howdee pappy."

"Howdee pappy."

"Oi don't know wha' mattah wit' dis' boy, ni. Comin' on de boat he was—"

"Come an' kiss me, sah."

He flinched at the suggestion. But there was no escape and he had to put up his face to receive the wet, disgusting kiss.

"Like yo' ent glad to see yo' pappy," he heard his mother say, and was ferocious at her, "an' bin talkin' an' exquirin' 'bout what yo' look like, Lucian, evah sense we lef' B'bados."

He slunk back, shuddering at the touch of the man, and took a good look at him. He was crouched before a machine. He was fairer than Sarah—she was black, he a yellowish

brown. He was soft, yet not fat, but he gave one the appearance of being weak and flabby. He was biting thread. Gold-
rimmed brown glasses barely shaded eyes circulating in two
seamy bloodshot pools. His hairy arms rested soft and heavy
on the machine. He was bald, and his mouth was large and
sensuous. It was a roaming mouth. His hands were of putty.
Every time he swallowed, or raised his head, a rum goggle as
modest as a turkey gobbler's would slide up and down.

The place was noisy and vulgar. It smelt of brandy and
Jamaica rum, but tuxedos and crash tunics were sewed there
for the dandy *bomberos* of the Republic. Far into the night it
kept twenty men on the job, but it was an idler's and a lazy
man's joint. Customers like the judge, a proud, blue-eyed
Spaniard, would stop by on their way home at night—but it
was a hang-out and an assignation spot for *cabrons* and barefooted black mares.

"Go an' pick up dah cotton reel fuh mah," Bright said to
him, "an' put dis empty bottle behind the counter—"

It was here that Gerald was to take on the color of life.

VI

"Mama, a las siete!"

It was seven o'clock. Anger, noise, confusion—a cock's
lofty crowing. Opening his eyes, he stood quietly, deciding.
In a tall bare room, he had been warmed in the night first by
one adult body, then, an eternity later, by another. Now he
was free of the sense of both.

A sun, immortal, barbaric as any reigning over Black
Rock, shot hazes of purple light on the evening's litter scat-
tered about.

"*Mama, a las siete!*"

Ah, he was not now on the ship. Nor was he at the tailor shop. This must be—home.

He sat up in bed, gazing at the enormity of things in the room. "Oh, Mama—" he cried, but no answer came. He jumped off the bed and dragged on his boots. He dressed and made for the door. He was struck once more by the glow of the bright Panama sun. The room opened out on a porch, not very wide, and there was no awning to cool it.

"*Mama, a las siete!*"

Down by the stairs a half-sick, half-clothed little child was crying. Standing above him was a lank, black, cruel-faced woman, brewing a cup of hot milk. As soon as the milk was shifted from one cup to the other, she would turn and stamp at the little boy on the floor.

"Where am I to get it from?" she screamed at him, "shut up, I say—shut up—before I cuff you—what do I care if you haven't eaten for two days—your stomach burning you— well go to sleep—you been already—well go again—sleep, sleep—it will do you good—it will make you forget you ever had a belly.

"Think I pick up smoked sausage? I've got to buy it. And what have I got to buy it with? Filth! May the heavens consume you! Shut up, I say! Who cares whether it is seven o'clock—or eight o'clock—or nine o'clock? Let me be! The baby's got to eat, and you'd better be gone, you're too noisy. Seven o'clock! Sing it to the birds, sing it to the canary, sing it to the winds. Winds can wake up the dead. Go try—bawl it to the winds! But I've got my own song, I've got my own tune. I don't want to hear you, shut up, I say."

All this in a tongue musical to Gerald, but the cries of

the little boy and the pox on his face and the sores making a batter of his toes unforgettably moved him.

At the cesspool he espied a girl. Her back was to him. She was of mixed blood, of assafetida brown, and had once had the smallpox. She was shouting at the top of her voice to the Chinaman downstairs to "giv' me wattah, yo' dam China-mang, you giv' me de wattah."

It took a long time for it to treacle upstairs. The water struggling up at last, she proceeded to bathe Madame's canary. To supervise the rite, Madame came herself—adding to the Cholo girl's swift parrot-like chatter words just as swift and as parrot-like.

Madame was a beauty. Wife of a Colombia rum merchant, she was fat and rosy and white. "Me white," she'd say to the West Indian lodgers in her tenement, "you no see fo' my skin?" The plate of her jeweled bosom soared high. Encountering it, one's first impulse would be not to lay one's head on it, but to cling, climb, sit safely and plumply on it. Her flat, wrinkled face had been smothered in some starch-like powder. She was white, as whites on the Isthmus went, but the flour or powder which she dabbed so thick on her face sometimes failed to accomplish its task. At intervals the wind or the latitudinous heat dissipated splotches of the starchy pallor, and Madame's neck, or the rim of Madame's mouth, or the balloons under Madame's eyes—would expose a skin as yellow as the breasts of the Cholo girl.

Mistress of the tenement, and using a row of six of its one-rooms, Madame's love of jewels rose to a fetish. Her suite was full of jewelry. Her opulent person was ablaze with them. Her bright, thick black hair was prickly with hairpins of silver, hairpins of gold. She wallowed in colors, too. Some of the pins were blue, some red, others green. Her fat, squat arms were loaded with bangles. Her gaping stomach shimmered in a sea of rich white silk. Walking, it rolled, and dazzled, and shimmered.

Waltzing by Madame and the Cholo girl, there sallied out of the kitchen a woman. She was a mulatto. She was carrying a smoking dish of stewed peas and her head was held high in the clouds. Squat as Madame, she, too, was mad about jewelry. Her arms were creased with bracelets. And no jewel-ankled Hindu maiden had finer nuggets of gold flung about her neck. Her clogged feet sent buxom out at you a belly bursting with a fat, mellow tumor.

She came clogging straight at Gerald, and smiled. One of the one-room flats on that side of the porch belonged to her, but on spying him she swept past it.

"Run down to the John Chinaman's like a good little boy and bring me a loaf of French bread and a tin of sardine—"

"Come, wash yo' face and drink yo' tea, Gerald, befo' it get cold," cried a voice.

"Orright, mama, ah comin'," and he ran away, uncertain of the escape, leaving the St. Thomas virgin with the *peso* in her hand, stumped.

Fired by the beauty of the marbles and the speed of the tops—gigs—he'd go on secret escapades to the alley below and spin gigs and pitch taws with the boys who'd gather there. He had to be careful of the *pacos*. He had to be careful of the boys he played with. Some of them used bad words; some had fly-dotted sores on their legs. A city of sores. Some of them had boils around their mouths. Some were pirates— they made bloody raids on the marbles.

One day he was alone spinning his gig. It was a particularly rhythmical one. It was pretty, too—for he had dabbed a bit of washblue on top of it so that it looked beautiful when it was spinning.

Suddenly a gang of boys came up, Spanish boys. One of them, seeing his top, circling and spinning, measured it; then winding his up, drew back and hauled away. The velocity released made a singing sound. Gerald stood back, awed. The top descended on the head of his with astounding accuracy and smashed it into a thousand pieces. The boys laughed, and wandered on.

At marbles some of the boys would cheat, and say, "if you don't like it, then lump it! *Chumbo!* Perro!" Some of them'd seize his taw or the marbles he had put up and walk away, daring him to follow. In the presence of all this, he'd draw back, far back, brooding. . . .

Sea on top of sea, the Empire mourned the loss of a sovereign; and to the ends of the earth, there sped the glory of the coronation.

Below Gerald's porch there spread a row of lecherous huts. Down in them seethed hosts of French and English blacks. Low and wide, up around them rose the faces and flanks of tenements high as the one Gerald lived in. Circling these one-room cabins there was a strip of pavement, half of which was shared by the drains and gutters. But from the porch, Gerald was unable to see the strip of pavement, for the tops of these huts were of wide galvanize, which sent the rain a foot or two beyond the slanting rim.

But it wasn't raining, the sun was shining, and it was the day of the queen's coronation. On that galvanized roof the sun bristled. Flaky, white—the roof burned, sizzled. The sun burned it green, then yellow, then red; then blue, bluish white, then brownish green, and yellowish red. It was a fluid, lustrous sun. It created a Garden of the roof. It recaptured the essence of that first jungle scene. Upward, on one of the roof's hills spread the leaves of banyan tree. Fruit—mellow, hanging, tempting—peeped from between the foliage of coffee and mango and pear. Sunsets blazed forth from beyond the river or the yellowing rice hills on some fertile roof.

All day, the day of the coronation, Gerald stood on the porch, peering down on the burning roof. It dazzled him, for up from it came sounds; sounds of music and dancing. Sounds of half-drunk creoles screaming, "*Sotie, sotie!*" Flutes and "steel" and hand-patting drums; fast, panting music, breathless, exotic rhythm; girls, with only a slip on, wild as larks, speeding out of this room, into that one. All day, the day of the coronation, the music lasted, the dancing lasted, the feeling mounted.

A slippery alley connected Bottle Alley and Bolivar Street. Through it Gerald tiptoed, surreptitiously, to see the *bomberos* on parade. He stood at the edge of the curb, gazing up the street at the clang and clash of red flannel shirts, white pants, brass helmets and polished black leggings. Behind him was a canteen and it was filled to its swinging half-sized doors with black upholders of the Crown. Gazing under a halfdoor he could see hosts of trousered legs vaguely familiar to him.

The coronation rags of the bar were a dark, somber kind. Dark-green leaves, black-green leaves—wreaths and wreaths of them.

"Come on, Dina, an' behav' yo'self. Yo' ain't gwine wine no mo' fi' suit any big teet' Bajan."

"Who is a big teet' Bajan?"

"Who yo' tink 's talkin' to? I didn't know yo' wuz hard a hearing."

"Bet yo' ah lick yo' down, if yo' go long talkin' like dat?"

"Say dah again, ni, betcha yo' don't say dah again."

"Look at dese two, ni. Wuh, Bright, yo' ort to be shame o' yo'self, man, fightin' ovah a chiggah foot gal."

"Who yo' callin' chiggah-foot? Me?"

"Oi ent talkin' to you, soul."

"Ah buss yo' head open fuh yo', yes, yo' go on playin' wit' my Trinidad uman! See dah stick in de corner—"

"Butt 'e! Butt 'e down! Don' lick 'e wit' de stick! Butt 'e down!"

"Wuh 'bout it?"

"Wuh 'bout it? Wait an' see!"

"Look out, Lucian, befo' he chop open yo' head."

"Oh mi Gahd!"

"H'm! Yo' beast! Yo' whelp! Leave my uman alone."

A figure, washed in blood, fell backwards through the half-door on to the refuse-littered pavement.

All night Sarah sat up, imploring the Lord to have mercy upon them, and beseeching Bright to mend his reckless ways. His head bandaged up, he lay on the bed, a ghastly figure, the pain crushing the fire out of his eyes.

"Yo' ort to tek dis as a warnin'," she said, "an' steady yo'self." And he only moaned in pain.

All night Gerald was restless, bruised by his mother's sorrow, and unable to rid himself of the hideous nightmares surrounding it.

In the morning the lodgers grew restive.

"Yo' heah all dah ruction las' night, Maria, like dey wuz bringing up a dead man up de stairs?"

"Oi taught dey was gwine break down de house—"

"No," flounced Maria, "no ask-ee fuh me, me no no."

"But ent yo' hear um, Miss Collymore? Ni?"

"No harm meant, soul—"

"Didn't you, Mrs. Bright?"

"Yes, I heard it."

"Wha'm wuz, ni? Yo' know?" All eyes were turned upon her. But she calmly responded, "It was my husband. He went to a ball given by the tailors and he must have had too much ice cream—"

"Yes?" some one tittered.

"Fuh true?"

"Yo' see, evah since he wuz home he liked to eat ice cream, but it don't agree wit' him—"

"Yo' don't say."

"No, it don't agree wit' he, an' he nose run blood like a stan'pipe run water. An' dey put 'e out 'pon the verandah fuh hol' 'e head back, and he fell asleep an' de moon shine 'pon 'e all night—"

"Oi had a boy who got de moon in he face, dah way, heself."

"Well, you know den. As I wuz—he sit dey all night wit' de moon shinin' in 'e face, wit' he head cocked back, an' when dey fomembah an' come out an' look at 'e dey fine 'e had one eye shut up, an' instead o' stoppin' de blood de moon only start it running wussah."

"Hey, we can't 'elp yo' wid 'e, ni, Miss Bright?"

"No, soul, Oi jess takin' dis fish tea fuh 'e. Dey say it is good fo' wash 'e eye wid. Dey say it will ca'y way de redness an' de soreness."

"G'long, soul, an' do yo' bes' fuh get 'e bettah."

Taking broth to him, she murmured, "Ain't yo' shame o' yo'self to hav' me bring yo' something to eat—"

"Oh, God, uman, don't torture me," he cried, tossing in misery and pain.

"Don't torture yu', ni, Oi mus' love yo'—is dah wha' yo' wan' me fuh do?"

"Oh, God, lemme 'lone," he cried, raving like a bull, "lemme bones rest in peace, ni?"

"Yo' scamp yo'! Yo' heart ort to prick yo' till yo' las' dyin' day fuh all yo' do to me an' my po' chirrun—"

"Oh, how many times I gwine heah de same old story?"

"Old? It will never be old! As long as I've got breath in my body—as long as I is got my boy child to shield from de worle—from de filth and disease of this rotten, depraved place—as long as I got my fo' gal chirrun in B'bados in somebody else han'—um can't be a old story!"

"Giv' me de t'ing, no," he cried, tired and exhausted, "if yo' gwine giv' me, an' le' me head res' in peace. Yo' don't know how bad it is hurtin' me now."

The day he was ready to go back to the shop, she said to him, "Tek heed, Lucian, yo' heah, yo' bes' tek heed, an' men' yo' ways—"

"O Jesus! jess because yo' been tendin' to me when I wuz sick, yo' think yo' gwine tell me wha' to do, ni, but yo' lie, uman, yo' lie!" and he sped downstairs, swanking, one eye red and flashing.

To the pirates and urchin gods of Bottle Alley, Gerald

was the bait that lured a swarm of felt-hatted *pacos* who kept the alley under sleepless surveillance. It was risky to loiter, play marbles, spin gigs—and there wasn't enough to keep Gerald occupied upstairs. So he hit upon the notion of going at dusk to his father's shop. There he'd gather rum bottles and cotton reels, open up the backyard and inveigle the Judge's son to come down and play shells—and shut his ears to the men's vile banter. . . .

One day, after the men had gone, he saw his father take a glass bowl from a shelf far back in the shop and put it on his machine. He was drawn to it, for, squirming about in the weed and moss, was a congeries of little black reptiles.

"Papa, wha' is dese, ni?"

"Leave them, sir!" his father shouted, "an' get away from there!"

He drew back, afraid. The place was silent. He watched his father furtively. His face was clouded, agitated, aflame. He tore off his coat, peeled back his shirt sleeve, and revealed a red, sore arm. He squeezed it, the while gritting his teeth. He moved over to the bowl, wincing in pain. Gerald was stricken dumb. Up to the bowl his father crept, taking one of the shiny, slimy reptiles and planting it on the red sore, to feast there. Uncomprehending Gerald patiently waited.

Later he was in bed, half-asleep, listening to the storm. A hurricane of words passed by—hot, carnal words. The fury subsided, and there ensued a sober sympathetic calm.

"Lucian, darling," he heard his mother say, "wha' yo' doin' fuh de arm, ni?"

"Oh, Oi is orright."

"Yo' bin to de doctor, man?"

"No."

"An' you mean to tell me yo' gwine sit down an' not do nutton fuh dah han' yo' got dey. Hey, man, yo' know wuh is good fo' yo'self?"

"Oh, Oi put a leech on it teeday. Dah ort to draw out all de bad blood."

As the nights advanced, the heat became more and more severe. It was useless to try to sleep. Body smells, body vapors, the room's need of oxygen—grew tense, exacting.

"Yo' know, Sarah, dis t'ing is really hurtin' me; why um is worse dan Oi taught um wuz. Um is stickin' me jess like a needle."

"H'm, tell yo' so—tell yo' yo' won't men' yo' ways."

"O Christ," he roared, "why yo' don't say yo' glad an' done?"

At Sixth and Hudson Alley there was a branch of the Plymouth Brethren, and Sarah suddenly went about the business of securing "acceptance" there. Now, so far as running it went, the shop was out of Bright's hands. He was ill, and had to stay at home. One of the men, Baldy, a mulatto Antiguan, took hold of things.

By way of the Sixth Street Mission, his mother rooted religion into his soul. Every night he was marched off to meeting. There, he'd meet the dredge-digging, Zone-building, Lord-loving peasants of the West Indies on sore knees of atonement asking the Lord to bring salvation to their perfidious souls. In the isles of their origin they were the tillers of the soil—the ones to nurture cane, and water sorrel, stew cocoanuts and mix Maube—now theirs was a less elemental, more ephemeral set of chores. Hill and vale, valley and stream gave way to wharf and drydock, dredge and machine shop. Among the women the transfiguration was less brilliant. Dull. The "drops" and cakes and foods and pops vended to the serfs and squatters on insular estates found a husky-throated market at the ends of the pay car lines.

Thursday night was prayer meeting. Religiously Sarah and Gerald went. All the brothers and the sisters took a deep and vital interest in him. They'd bring him sweets, and coppers, and stare long at him, their eyes wet, and soft. They came, a drove of them, to the house, all dressed in black, which set the neighbors talking.

He was not a child of the Lord, he did not believe in the Scripture, but it did not serve to rob them of their sense of charity. So they came to see, and give words of courage to the family of the sick man. They'd read passages of the Bible to him, and marvel at the priceless wonders of Christ Jesus. And then one day he said to her, "Sarah, I think I ort to go to the horspitral—I can't see—my eyes is painin' me so bad. Oi wondah wha' is de mattah wit' dem."

"Didn't de medicine de doctah giv' yo' do yo' any good, Lucian?"

"Oh, that bitter t'ing? Good wha'! Oi feel like Oi could cut off this bleddy old han'—"

"It still hurtin' yo, Lucian?"

"Cuttin' me like a knife."

After they came and got him, Gerald began to feel things ever so much more keenly. His vision, too, grew less dim. But a pallor fell on things. In the morning he went to the cesspool to whistle to the canary while the Cholo girl washed it. But as he approached she fled in terror screaming "No, no, don't touch—go 'way—yo' no good—no clean—me no like yo' no mo'." The little boy, the seven o'clock one, refused to let him come near him. "No, no," he also cried, "me mama no like—" None of the old gang, who'd been willing to elude or defy the *pacos* and foregather down in the alley came any more. And he didn't go to the shop, either. It was so dark and silent over there. Only Baldy looked on—all the other men, one by one, had gone to other places to work. Dust grew high, thick. Spiders spun webs on the very frame of the door.

But he went oftener to the Sixth Street Mission, he and Sarah. The folks there weren't fickle—firm, solid, lasting. His mother had become one of them. He was one of them now. He'd go on Thursday evenings to prayer meetings. The evenings were long and hot. He would go to sleep in the midst of some drowsy exhaustless prayer. All would be silent. Hours of silence to God. Then they'd rise, slowly, back-crackingly, and he'd be left kneeling, snoring. He would be immune to pinches, nudges, murmurs. They'd be useless, he would be fast asleep. His mother'd pinch him, quietly, but he'd be as stiff as a log till the service was over.

All in black—veil, hat, gloves, shoes, dress.

At Sixth and Bolivar they took one of those modest subdued coaches, not adorned by any wig-powdered Jamaican Pretty Socks, and bade the driver take them to the city hospital.

The sun dealt the city some stern body blows. The piazzas were strewn with folk. Bees and flies and fleas sang and buzzed and added to the city's noise and squalor. Swinging onto rafts hoisted high on porches parakeets and parrots screeched and chattered incessantly. In cages set in the shades of windows bright-feathered and trill-voiced birds languished half-sleepily. Down on the piazza among the old women and the children the Duque ticket sellers and the sore-footed heathens, there were monkeys. Tied to poles greasy and black with banana grime they were lathering their faces with spit. Slowly they ascended the head of the street, the chapel of the Christ Church, felt a bit of the onrushing sea wind and made the drive. The sea wind beat against them. It was cool and refreshing. At last they were at the hospital.

A high box, square, gauze-encased and white with a dim black object in it was set at the end of a back porch—wide, long, screened, isolated. Facing it was a planted plot, gardened by Asiatics, seen through the dusty screen. Near the sloping end of the porch the rosebush was withering; mocking the bitter fury of the sun the sunflowers were slightly bowing. Accustoming one's eye to the dead reach of things beyond the screen one saw a terra-cotta sky and lank, parched trees with reddish-brown foliage. One saw, sizzling, at the mouths of dying flowers, blue-winged humming birds—

An eternity had passed since the doctor had brought them there, and all the sorrow and anguish inside her rushed to Sarah Bright's eyes.

"Yo' mus' pray fuh me, Sarah," were the first words that came to her from the box square.

"Yes, Lucian," she said, concurring in their finality.

He emitted a groan, and she patted Gerald's face, forcing the child to look away.

"An' wuh duh say, Lucian," she asked, with piety and anxiety, "wuh duh say, ni?"

Their eyes were fastened on the fixed intensity of the sun, but their ears were attuned to the tiniest rustle of the glazed sheets, and the restless figure under them. Then he said, "Ah'm in a bad way, gyrl."

She took out a little white handkerchief and dried first Gerald's mouth and nose, then her own glistening eyes.

He groaned, and was restive again. "De doctah say no use—de oil ent no good."

"No?" there was a quiet suspense in her voice.

"No bloomin' good!" he flung, unearthing some of the old asperity.

"Don't, Lucian," she entreated, "fomembah Jesus."

"Oh, God, dis han'!" he groaned, tossing fiercely.

He ruffled the sheets, and a lizard, a big lanky bark-hued one, slid down the trunk of the cocoanut tree, after some gawkier prey.

"An' dey ent try nutton else," she said, again exhuming the handkerchief.

"Oh, dese Yankees don't cyah wuh de do to yo'—dey don't cyah. Duh wouldn't even giv' yo' a drop o' hot wattah, if yo' ask me. No, dey ent try nutton else."

"Hush, don't cry, Gerald," she said, hunting for a piece of Chinese candy, "yo' mustn't cry, son."

"An' wuh dey gwine do, Lucian," she said, reluctantly risking the query.

"Put me 'way—Palo Seco—dah's de colony."

"Don't cry, son, never min', mamma will tek care o' Gerald—oh, my son, you'll break my heart."

"'E love 'e pappy, ent 'e?" he smiled, then turned his moistening eyes to the black wall behind him.

"Well," she said, her eyes clear and dry, "the Lord wuks His wonders in a mysterious way. What's to be, will be."

He, too, was weeping; but she held on, driving the mirage to the winds.

"Yo' kin come to see muh, Sarah," he said, "dey allow yo' one visit a year—yo' mus' come, yo' hear?"

"Yes, Lucian, I'll come."

"An' yo' mustn't call me bad, yo' heah?" he pleaded, the water in his eyes, like a young culprit.

"God forbid, dear—be quiet now. Come, Gerald, time fi' go, son." She adjusted his hat, and a bell started ringing.

"An' yo' mus' tek good cyah o' yo'self, heah Sarah, an' don't le' nobody tek exvantage o' yo', yo' heah, dis is a bad country—"

"Yes, Lucian."